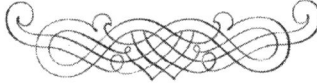

All Rights Reserved

Published by Five Pyramids Press, Suite 1a 34 West Street,
Retford, England, DN22 6ES
ISBN: 9798274731836

RAPINE

Emmy Ellis

Chapter One

The November damp had seeped into London, clinging to the grimy brickwork of the buildings, the puddles iced in the alleyways and gutters. That dampness matched the air inside Amelia Bagby's café, which had a cloying humidity in it, something she did on purpose. She kept the place too warm and put bowls of water in various places so the windows were always fogged with condensation.

She didn't want certain people seeing inside. The police. The twins.

She'd been running the place for far too long. Decades. In her seventies now, she'd seen London move through the ages, and a lot of the time she'd been desperately unhappy, pretending everything was okay when it most certainly wasn't. Now that she was older and could look back on her life through a different lens, she wished she'd had more courage to stand up for what was right. But society back then was nothing like it is now; during her most trapped period, women had to do as they were told.

Such a shame that she'd let those rules continue throughout the years. It was as if she was stuck back there, unable to move past it. Not to say that she was happy now either. Most of the time these days, she didn't like what she saw; modern criminals weren't a patch on those in her heyday. And most of the time, she didn't like how she felt. Still trapped, but she had no one to blame for it this time round except herself.

Her café had no name. No sign out the front. Most people didn't even know coffee and sandwiches were served inside. Normal people were discouraged. Amelia kept the place tatty on purpose so that if someone off the street walked in, they'd see the dirty tables and floor and back away quickly.

She'd run this criminal establishment for years without any leaders poking their noses in, and she didn't intend for that to change. The men who came in knew not to say a word about what went on here. They'd be stupid if they did—they'd lose their safe space to chat. She charged them a fee to do so, which included all the hot drinks they wanted, plus a sandwich. If she wasn't here, then they all helped themselves, or her friend, Shank, kept things running for her. She'd only ever be in the flat above anyway, close enough that if someone called, she'd be there in a jiffy. The one hundred pounds a day each person paid her was worth its weight in gold to them. It was private here, or as private as they made it, considering the tables were usually always full and every single 'customer' had ears.

Most conversations went on in whispers.

This was no place for polite society. Men huddled at the tables—some of them with hard eyes and sharp suits, although the new breed coming up had tracksuit bottoms and hoodies, their laughter too loud, their smiles too wide, their privilege shining. She couldn't stand the little bastards if she were honest, but money was money, and she had a living to earn.

Or an escape fund to build up.

Her customers were here for the anonymity, the unspoken understanding that what was said within these walls stayed there. If anyone was found passing on overheard information, or using it for their own ends, then they weren't welcome here anymore.

Shank, a man whose profile was as familiar to her as her own reflection, sat at a table in the corner, his back to the wall. His frame was still lean, though the years had etched lines around his eyes and a permanent divot between his eyebrows. He cradled a cup, although it had to be empty by now.

Amelia got up and went behind the counter with its baskets of sugar sachets, wooden stirrers, and tray of condiments. She made a pot of tea—so much easier these days with the hot water urn she'd had installed—and popped it on a tray along with a little jug of milk, two cups, and four sachets of sugar. She carried it over to Shank's table and placed it down, and because of her shaking hands, the cups slid together and clinked.

She hated these little reminders that she was getting older.

She sat opposite him. He met her gaze, a faint smirk playing on his lips, a ghost of the man he once was. So much had happened between them that by rights, she shouldn't let him come in here, she should have told him, many moons ago, to sling his fucking hook and never come back. But she never had mastered the art of doing what was best for her. She'd always deferred to the men in her life, even to her own detriment.

She regretted it now, but it wasn't too late to fix it. She had maybe ten years left in which she could live a life just for herself. All she needed was a little bit more money to do it. Would it be weird to move away from London? Of course it would, it was all she'd ever known, but a change was as good as a rest, so they say, and by God, she needed a rest.

"What's up?" Shank asked as he took the liberty of pouring their teas. His hands didn't shake like hers.

"It's been ages, and I have didn't seen hide nor hair of that Floyd lad."

"I wondered when you were going to bring him up. I thought you were losing your marbles, what with not mentioning him, especially because of the discussion we had."

Last month, Amelia had broached a certain subject with Shank, needing his help on a job she had in mind, but she'd wanted to wait a few weeks before they embarked on it, so it wouldn't look like she'd overheard information in the café and used it for her own ends. Broken her own rule. That would be exactly what happened, but it didn't mean people had to know that.

She took a sip of her tea, the scalding liquid burning a path down her throat.

"Do you think he got himself in a bit of trouble and that's why he hasn't been in?" Shank asked.

"The only trouble I want that kid in is the trouble we cause him." She smiled. "Do you remember they *why* of what we talked about?"

Shank nodded, his eyes never leaving hers. "One last dance in the darkness."

"A final hurrah," Amelia said, a spark igniting inside her. "Before the dust settles for good over my coffin. I need to feel it, Shank. One last time. The rush. The blood pumping. I want to feel young again."

She'd said all this to him before, and he'd responded that he was too old for this shit, and nowadays, he was the one who set the jobs up and got other people to do them for him. He claimed the days of going out there and feeling alive were long gone, but she'd persuaded him that the job she had in mind wasn't going to get his heart rate spiking too much, and no one was going to suspect two old people of relieving a man of the burden of a suitcase full of cash.

She'd spent too many years as a ghost, drifting through the days. Partly her own doing, especially once the eighties rolled around and people weren't so judgmental, but by then she'd got herself stuck in a rut and had accepted her life wasn't going to amount to much beyond what she did now. Back in the sixties, it had been so different, where she'd had to follow men's rules and do as she was told. She could have rebelled, but she'd long since known that deep down she was weak-willed, despite the occasional fire that roared inside her.

So, the idea of one last job had come about. She wanted to chase the electric hum that had coursed through her veins when she was young, when life felt like a series of dares and possibilities—but wasn't she lying to herself there? It wasn't excitement but fear. Did she really want to feel *that* again?

Amelia leaned closer, dropping her voice. "Floyd. Talked a bit too loose in here, didn't he. I mean, what kind of prat tells another criminal he has cash hidden in a suitcase? He's lucky it was me who overheard, me who plans to rob him, because anyone else would give him a good bash over the head to knock him out."

"*We* plan to rob him, you mean."

"Yes, we."

The suitcase money must have come from deals she'd assumed Floyd talked about with his brother, Simon, who'd lived in Grove Manor, although he'd gone 'missing' and Floyd now lived there.

Shank's eyebrows quirked. "We never did get down to the nitty-gritty of planning this out. What are we doing, going to the manor, finding the suitcase, then just fucking off with it? Assuming we even find it."

Amelia took another sip of tea. "That's the plan."

Shank let out a low whistle. "How long are we giving ourselves to search the place?"

"A couple of hours."

He snorted. "I looked it up, the manor. Built last century. Full of nooks and crannies. We might need more than a couple of hours."

She'd looked it up, too, and her mind had already mapped it out. The layout, the vulnerabilities. She'd seen enough of Floyd in this very café to build a dossier in her head of who he was. He was overly brash at times, but maybe that was something he did for show. Maybe he felt he had to fight to be seen here amongst the others who were clearly much more confident than him. He could be doing it to fit in. Everyone had vulnerable spots, didn't they. Anyway, she reckoned he was the perfect mark.

Except for one thing. He'd done time for murder.

The thing was, there was nothing scary about him. She wasn't bothered if he tried to find whoever had robbed him and ended up on her doorstep. All right, she'd be worried if he put his hands around her neck, but she had her late husband's gun upstairs, and she'd use it if she had to.

"Can you imagine what Lenny would have to say about this?" Shank asked.

Why did he have to go and bring *him* up? A bitter taste flooded her mouth. Lenny, the man whose words had kept her caged for years, frightened, anxious, worried that if she flew the nest he'd come after her and make sure she disappeared forever. He'd had such a hold on her, and now he was dead and gone, she often wondered why on earth she'd been scared of him. Time had erased some of the memories, or at least shaved the worst bits off, so that she no longer remembered the harsher things he'd done.

Actually, she remembered them well enough, she just didn't allow herself to wallow in the feelings she'd once felt.

Everyone used to think they were devoted to each other, but it had been an illusion. The mourners at his funeral had clucked sympathetically, praising her unwavering loyalty, how she'd cared for him when he'd been dying. They had no idea she'd wanted to place a pillow over his face and suffocate the wanker for everything he'd put her through. For making her so scared of him she'd put *herself* through it. She'd nodded, accepted their condolences, forcing tears at just the right moments.

But the truth, raw and ugly but justified, was that she'd hated him.

He'd been a constant, suffocating weight—a grey, damp blanket draped over every flicker of joy or ambition she'd had. Her hatred for him had been an insidious worm feeding on her soul, chomping away. The life he'd offered her had turned into a custodial sentence.

Many a time, she'd wished him dead. That dark wishing hadn't been fleeting; it had become a permanent fixture. She'd privately cultivated it, tending the hatred like a rare, toxic bloom. It was an act of self-preservation, a way to get through. Back then, if she'd stopped hating him, she'd have to admit she'd wasted years of her life in stagnant misery, and that thought was unbearable. The hatred proved he was the problem, that he was the one in the wrong.

She didn't hate Lenny anymore. She'd grown up and realised hatred was wasted energy, and she had none to spare for a ghost. What she felt now was a deep, quiet sadness for the young woman she'd been—the woman who'd put her life into dry dock, waiting for the harsh tide of Lenny's presence to recede.

She'd had dreams once. Wild, impossible dreams of adventure, of living a life less ordinary. Instead, she'd lived a life less ordinary, but it wasn't quite what she'd envisaged. He'd wrapped invisible chains around her, binding her to a life she'd grown to despise. In the end he'd sucked the air out of everything. Nowadays he'd be called a fun sponge. She preferred to just call him a cunt.

She'd stayed with him. For appearances, for the hope that things would change, for the crippling embarrassment of what people would say if she left. Divorce was scandalous then, a stain that couldn't be scrubbed away. You didn't just leave your husband. You endured. And she had, for too many excruciating years.

She wished she'd walked out one day and never looked back, consequences be damned. But she hadn't, and the resentment had festered. Every year that passed, every shared meal, every forced smile, every empty word, hacked at her soul.

Thank God he's dead.

"I don't give a fuck *what* Lenny would have thought," she said.

She looked at Shank, his eyes meeting hers, understanding already etched there. He knew her, perhaps better than he should, certainly better than Lenny ever had. He knew what she'd been through. He was the only one, apart from herself and Lenny, who did.

"So," she said, "the manor, the suitcase. We need to talk shop."

Shank nodded, a glint in his eye. "Right."

For the first time in years, Amelia felt alive. The café and its criminals blurred into the background. All that mattered was the exhilarating promise of one last dance with danger.

She couldn't wait.

Chapter Two

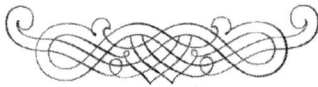

1965

*H*ome from work after a long day behind the counter in Woolworths, her feet aching, seventeen-year-old Amelia kicked off her shoes, tossing her bag on her bed. She glanced at the clock on the wall; she had just under two hours before Brenda came round to walk with her to a party. Aching feet or not, *she'd still stand on them all night if it meant having a good time. She was determined to throw herself into it tonight. Normally she was a bit of a wallflower. She'd dig deep to get some courage, then see where the night took her.*

Since she was almost eighteen, Mum and Dad had been giving her a bit more leeway on how long she stayed out, but most of the time, she and Brenda pretended to be staying at each other's houses when really they hung around at parties until the morning. Once, in the summer, they even slept in a field, the sky a weird grey and no stars in sight. She wanted to live a little, be a bit more dangerous. See who she really was. It was the sixties, for crying out loud, and the possibilities were endless. Anyway, Amelia reckoned Mum and Dad were happy for her to go out because it meant she was more likely to meet a bloke. If she did that, they'd encourage her to get married and move out.

Mum seemed to think that was an ambition Amelia had to fulfil. Marriage, a house, children, a dog. A man who came home every Friday after a long week of working to keep a roof over their heads and gave her a bunch of flowers, a box of chocolates if she was really lucky.

Apparently, that was all she needed to look forward to.

A shiver of excitement ran through her. Everyone had been talking about this party, seeing as there'd be booze and unlimited cigarettes. The bloke who was throwing it, Malcolm, was the type who had money to burn and was spending time living in a downmarket, lower-class house in the East End to give himself some 'life experience' on how the poor lived. She'd be offended if it wasn't so comical. When she'd first met him she'd expected him to be a posh ponce who didn't have a clue how people like her managed, but he'd surprised her by being generous and kind. She felt sorry for him in a way; everyone used him for his parties, the drink, and the ciggies, never really taking much notice of who he really was.

She imagined drinking gin, doing the twist, and having a slow dance with someone at the end. In the past, those dances had never gone anywhere other than the bloke fondling her bum, but she could hope for more, couldn't she? Maybe a kiss, a touch of her boob, and a promise for them to go on a date.

She placed a stack of 45s on the turntable, the crackle and pop of the needle dropping onto a record filling her small bedroom; she turned the volume down. Last time she'd had it loud because Mum and Dad had gone out.

While the music played, she dug through her jewellery box, scanning her collection of cheap bangles and earrings that she'd got off the market. She pictured the dance area — a square of living room floor — and the lads with their slicked-back hair, the girls in their finest. She deliberated between her yellow minidress and a black-and-white one she'd worn a fortnight ago. The yellow won; tonight she wanted to stand out. She slipped it on, pairing it with her white knee-high boots, the patent leather reflecting the light. They'd cost her a fortune, but she bet Malcolm could afford them without batting an eyelid.

She backcombed sections of her dark-brown hair, each strand coaxed into place. Then came the generous cloud of hairspray, a sweet-smelling fog that promised to hold her beehive in place. She drew dramatic, upturned wings with her eyeliner, then came the false eyelashes, thick and spidery. Blue eyeshadow added a touch of bold colour, and pale-pink lipstick completed her transformation. A final once-over in the mirror, and she smiled, dabbing her favourite perfume behind her ears. Grabbing her small, geometric-patterned bag, she made sure her mirror, lipstick, and some money were inside, along with her key.

A loud knock on the front door had her rushing to the window to peer down into the street. The redheaded Brenda stood on the cobbles staring up at her, gesturing at Amelia to get a move on. Amelia ran downstairs and opened the door. Brenda had moved forward to stand on the step in the same boots as Amelia, but she'd chosen a lime-green dress. Excitement bubbled up, and they grinned at each other.

"See you later, Mum!" Amelia shouted, getting outside quick so she wasn't called back in.

They legged it along the street, giggling, ignoring Mum yelling for them to come back so they could talk about where they were going. There was no way Amelia would be telling her that. The last thing she wanted was her parents turning up at the party later, at eleven o'clock, saying it was time to go home. The days of curfews were long gone now, but it seemed sometimes they forgot that.

On the way, Brenda passed on some gossip from Woolworths. "I heard some lads talking, so I looked up to see who they were, and one of them winked at me. I told them about the party tonight, so hopefully they'll be going."

"I wish I could be as confident as you with boys."

19

"You can be, you just get in your own way, I've told you that before. And I've also told you that nobody knows you're not confident unless you show that to them. Walk into a party like you own the place, that's my motto."

They reached the house, people standing around, smoking. The air hummed with chatter and music drifting from the open front door, beckoning guests into the lively scene. The front garden had been transformed. Strands of lights, looped through the branches of an oak tree, cast a gentle glow, highlighting the bob 'of balloons tied to the gate, announcing the party to the entire street. Amelia's first thought was that the neighbours wouldn't be too happy about Malcolm throwing a party, but then she remembered what he'd said before, that if you invited them then they were less likely to complain, even if they chose not to go.

Inside, the scent of cigarette smoke and cheap perfume hung a bit too heavy, and she coughed. The stairs were full of people sitting and talking, drinking and smoking. Conversations collided, layer upon layer. Amelia paused in the living room doorway, her eyes adjusting to the kaleidoscope of colours.

Malcolm, who had an avant-garde streak, gave them a nod. He leaned against a wall papered in swirls *of black and white. The opposite wall exploded with oversized flowers in pinks, oranges, and yellows. The furniture was modern, the kind Amelia would want in her house when she finally moved out of home. Low teak coffee tables, sideboards covered in bottles of spirits and overflowing ashtrays, the modular seating a burnt-orange and olive-green patterned fabric. The parquet floor would look nice with a shaggy rug on it.*

Couples danced in the small space near the record player. The girls' skirts swirled around their knees, revealing glimpses of bare skin higher up, while the men, in their slim-fit suits, moved less fluidly, like they weren't drunk enough to fully let go and enjoy themselves. Most of them were probably on the prowl, desperate to give a good impression.

Amelia took a drink from a passing tray—Malcolm hadn't quite left his posh world behind; women breezed by in waitress uniforms, their skirts so short their bum cheeks were on show. Amelia took a sip of bubbly and let the room's energy wash over her. Everyone seemed to be lit up in this noisy, smoke-filled room. If she were completely honest, she felt a bit out of her depth in places like this, and with Brenda nowhere to be seen, it looked like she had to make the best of it on her own.

Her attention drifted to a man by the black-and-white wall. He watched everyone, a half-empty glass in his hand. Tall and broad-shouldered, he filled out his navy-blue suit jacket nicely. His dark hair caught the light in a way that it looked almost black. His eyes got to her the most, a light shade of green, and they had an intensity that drew her. He raised his glass to his mouth, took a sip, and his gaze met hers over the rim. It was direct and held a hint of amusement, as if he knew she was only playing at being an adult. He didn't look away, didn't offer a polite nod or a forced smile, just stared.

Her heart banged faster, and a blush heated her neck. He pushed off the wall and approached—oh fuck!—and a knot of apprehension formed in her stomach. A sixth sense warning her to keep away from him? He seemed far too mature for her. Not that he was that much older or anything, but he had an air about him where he'd lived and she hadn't. Not properly anyway.

He stopped in front her. "Mind if I steal you away?"

Amelia swallowed, a shiver running through her. "Only if you promise to return me in one piece," she managed, her voice steadier than she felt. Had that sounded stupid? Would he think she was childish? God, she had no idea how to flirt.

He chuckled and extended a hand. "Lenny."

"Amelia." She placed her hand in his.

His grip was firm, warm, the skin smooth. So he wasn't a brickie or a carpenter then, or anyone who used his hands like that. Maybe he worked in an office. He led her away from the main throng to the large bay window, where a collection of tall potted ferns and a drinks globe offered privacy. They tucked themselves behind the leaves, and Lenny drew the curtains so the people in the front garden couldn't stare in at them. She wasn't sure whether she ought to be worried or pleased that he'd hidden her.

To her surprise, the conversation between them flowed effortlessly. They talked about music, the whacky wallpaper, politics. Lenny was sharp and perceptive. He spoke of his work in investment, which sounded vague, but she didn't know him well enough to press for more—or feel confident to.

In the background, the party pulsed with vibrant energy. While Lenny chattered on, Amelia glanced between the greenery at the room. Tucked away on the far end of the sofa, a woman in a daringly short shift dress drank something with ice in it, her gaze fixed on the man beside her. They looked so comfortable together.

Amelia hoped to have a relationship like that one day.

She focused back on Lenny. He was eloquent, charming even, as he wove tales of his burgeoning career, his role in 'shaping tomorrow', whatever that meant. And as his voice swelled, filling the space with the grand narrative of his own significance, she found her mind drifting, wondering what her tomorrow might look like beyond the polite confines of this conversation.

He must have seen he was losing her interest, because he changed tack, lightening the mood a little.

Half an hour later, Amelia found herself laughing more than she had in months, drawn into his orbit, mesmerised by his expressions, the way his lips curved when he smiled, the crinkling at the corners of his eyes. Maybe he wasn't such a bragger after all. The only thing she couldn't get over was why he was bothering to speak to her. She'd heard enough times, out of her mother's own mouth, that she was a face only her parents could love. Amelia was well aware she wasn't pretty, unlike Brenda who was stunning. But she had other things to offer. Mum had taught her to cook and sew, and she was good at cleaning, all things apparently required by a man before they took a woman on. Maybe Lenny had sensed she was more than just a plain face.

Hours dissolved. She forgot all about Brenda, who'd likely be busy with those lads she'd spoken to in Woolworths. It happened like this sometimes, where Brenda fucked off, and usually Amelia sat on her own in a corner, watching the goings-on, too shy to dip a toe in and see if she liked the water.

The party surged and ebbed, people came and went, but she and Lenny remained anchored in their quiet space. They danced once, his hand firm on her waist, and she hadn't stepped on his shoes.

Then, as it always did, the night waned, the music softened, and the crowd thinned. People slow-danced, and she held her breath, hoping Lenny would draw her to him to do the same, but he was intent on lighting a cigarette. The air, though still smoky, felt cooler— someone had opened a window, and a breeze blew through.

Lenny turned to her. "Can I see you home?"

Her heart thundered. Now, he was either being polite and gentlemanly or he wanted to wait until he was on her doorstep before he kissed her. "Okay, but I need to see if my friend's ready to go yet."

She spotted a crack in his almost perfect façade. He frowned—so he didn't like the idea of her having a friend? She brushed it off as him being disappointed that they might not end the evening alone in an alley somewhere. God, what was she thinking? She hoped she was worth more than some shadowy hideaway.

She found Brenda snogging Malcolm on a patchwork sofa in the kitchen, her leg draped over his waist, the expanse of her thigh on show, and his hand clamped possessively on her backside. Was this what Brenda got up to at parties? No wonder her lipstick was always smudged by the end of the night. Or in the morning.

"Um, Bren, I'm going now," Amelia said.

"I'm staying," Brenda slurred. "My mum thinks I'm round yours."

"Right."

Brenda laughed for no reason, her head thrown back, her throat exposed. How much had she had to drink? Should she take Brenda home with her?

Amelia thought about Lenny, and the decision made itself. "Will you look after her?" she asked Malcolm.

"Yep. She'll be fine here." He gestured to the people who still remained. "Him over there has got a *car if she decides she wants a lift to yours, but as far as I'm concerned, she's welcome to stay the night."*

"What a lovely boy you are, Malc," Brenda babbled.

Amelia left them to it.

The walk was so calm compared to the party's noisy energy. The streets, usually alive with kids playing out in the daytime and their mums nagging over fences, were quiet, bathed in the glow from lampposts. A breeze rustled through the trees, carrying the scent of exhaust fumes, the East End's perfume. Their footsteps echoed, and each tap reminded Amelia they hadn't said a word and time was running out. She'd be home before she knew it.

Was it normal for a bloke to walk someone home and not speak?

They reached her doorstep. Lenny faced her, the light from the nearby streetlamp illuminating the planes of his face, the intensity of his eyes. She held her breath, but he didn't make a move to kiss her, just looked at her, as if committing every detail of her features to memory. Or maybe she hoped *that was what he was doing. She grew uncomfortable. If she were pretty, she'd feel fine about him staring, but…*

"I've had a lovely night," he said.

"I have, too." Heat scored her cheeks, and they prickled.

And it was weird, standing on the cobbles, but Amelia knew she'd marry him. It was as if the knowledge had always been inside her but had only just come to light.

He leaned in then and brushed his lips over hers. "Goodnight, Amelia."

He stepped back, gave her one more look, then disappeared into the shadows of the street. Amelia's heart pounded, and a sense of having met her destiny bloomed inside her. Or was she being daft, as poetic as Malcolm could be? But she knew her life had changed tonight. She would marry Lenny, and though the road ahead might be uncharted, right now, she was certain she was exactly where she was meant to be.

Chapter Three

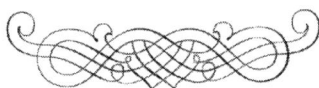

The wind scoured the skeletal branches of the trees lining Floyd Fleece's parents' street. A thin, persistent drizzle fuzzed the edges of the council houses. Each identical brick box, with its patch of lawn and old Sky dishes bolted to the chimneys, seemed to huddle together against the greyness, united in their agreement that the weather was piss-poor.

Floyd pulled the collar of his expensive, charcoal-grey coat tighter. Well, it was his now, but it hadn't always been. The weight of it always reminded him of the life his brother, Simon, had inhabited, and which Floyd had taken over. The manor house anyway. The coat didn't belong on him, too posh for the kid who'd grown up playing football on cracked pavements or kicking it against graffiti-scarred walls. He had a touch of impostor syndrome whenever he had it on, and Simon would have been livid if he knew he was wearing it.

Picture this: a man moving through life in someone else's clothes, not just a bit ill-fitting but fundamentally wrong. That's exactly how he felt, a perpetual stranger in his own skin, where every gesture and expression seemed like a stage act rather than his natural self. There was a constant itch of discomfort beneath his everyday existence, a persistent longing to feel truly at home in himself.

He doubted her ever would.

He sighed and stared around. This street hadn't changed much over the years. The primary school at the end still harboured screaming kids at playtime. The corner shop sold cut-price food behind its windows covered in posters showing eggs by the dozen and loaves of bread. When Floyd had come out of prison, seeing everything the same here had been a massive comfort; as for the rest of the things he'd seen, people and areas had moved on while he'd festered in his cell. Mind you, *he'd* changed over the years, too. It was impossible not to when your life was regimented, when you were institutionalised and living among some of the most savage animals on the planet.

Floyd was a murderer, but not the same type as the others.

He stared at number seventeen, where a mate of his had once lived. Net curtains hung in the living room, the pleats perfect. A plastic Father Christmas, prematurely festive, hung on the front door. He briefly wondered who lived there now but decided he didn't care. The past was the past, and he wasn't looking that way.

He took a deep breath, the cold air stinging his lungs, and walked up his parents' path. Pressed the doorbell. Braced himself to play the game of charades they'd been playing for the past month.

Mum opened the door, her face full of worry lines. Her eyes lit up when she saw him, as they always had. Simon had been convinced that Floyd was her favourite and could do no wrong. Even when Floyd had killed that girl, they'd stuck by him, Simon convinced nothing would make them stop loving him, but he hadn't known what had gone on in the background. He hadn't known that his parents had a big hand in Floyd ending up in prison.

Favourite or not, they'd done the right thing.

"Floyd, love, come in, you'll catch your death." She ushered him inside, her hand briefly touching his arm.

The warmth of the hall enveloped him. "Morning, Mum." He hung his coat on the overstuffed rack.

Dad was in the living room, holding a mug of tea, a newspaper spread over his lap. He looked up, his gaze heavy, tired. Maybe he didn't want to play charades anymore either. "Floyd. You took your time."

"Traffic." Floyd sat on the sofa. "You know what it's like."

Mum came in in with a steaming mug that she'd likely poured from a full pot, heading for the side table and setting it on a coaster. She gestured to it, then at Floyd, to let him know it was for him. She sat on the edge of the sofa, her hands clasped around her knees.

The silence, full of unspoken questions, got on Floyd's nerves. He knew what she wanted to talk about. He'd driven through the miserable London morning to deliver the same hollow reassurance he'd been dishing out to her for weeks, but fucking hell, he wished he didn't have to.

"Any news on the Simon fiasco?" Dad asked for her, his voice rough, attention still on the paper, although he wasn't reading it.

Floyd took a sip of tea. "I've been calling everyone who might know him, just like I said. His mates, his contacts…no one's seen him."

It was a lie. He hadn't called anyone. He pretended, every time he came here, that his brother was missing. He knew exactly where Simon was, and he wasn't breathing, put it that way.

After everything had happened, Floyd had gone to Simon's manor house. Even though he'd known the twins had sent a crew in to clean the mess up—the signs of the gunfight, the blood— he'd still been surprised to find it appeared as if nothing untoward had happened there at all. It had smelled of fresh paint and bleach. He'd walked through the silent rooms, imagining himself living there. He'd stayed, of course, someone had to look after the place. Someone had to make out they were keeping it aired and tidy for when Simon came home. For four weeks now, he'd been living in that big house as if he owned it, the bills coming out of his brother's bank account.

"It's been a month," Mum whispered. "A whole month. Not a call. Not a text."

"Which isn't unusual for him," Dad said. "Simon never really bothered with us the last few years. And I'm sick of this…this bullshit. We're sitting here like we don't know what happened to him. It's bloody obvious what went on. We told Floyd, when he found out what Simon had been up to with doing those godawful operations, stealing people's *organs*, for fuck's sake, that he should do the right thing, and then Simon disappeared."

Mum closed her eyes. She knew, she just didn't want to admit it out loud, so they'd continue to play this game.

Floyd glanced at his dad and shook his head—*don't upset her*. "He's probably taking a break in Cheltenham still. Maybe he needed to get away from everything for a bit."

"What about you?" Dad asked. "What's going on with you now?"

"I can handle myself," Floyd said. "I did as I was told, so no one will come and bother me." He meant the twins. He'd worked with them to bring Simon in, he'd known they were going to kill him, but he'd been desperate to save his own arse.

"Do you know what happened?" Mum asked. "There's nothing worse than not knowing if he's alive or dead."

Floyd flinched at the word 'dead'. "I don't know, I wasn't involved." *Fucking liar*. "And they told me not to discuss anything, so I can't."

"I'm hoping they've banished him," Mum said.

Dad sighed. "Banished?"

"Yes, banished. Sent him out of London, told him not to come back. They do that, don't they."

EMMY ELLIS

To keep Mum from tormenting herself, Floyd seized on the idea. It was a narrative that explained Simon's absence without revealing the brutal truth. "That's possible. It fits with how he seemed to just vanish. If he'd been told to leave, he'd probably been told to go completely off the grid, not tell anyone, even us, that he'd gone."

Dad considered it. He'd always been in the 'murdered' camp until now. "So he's in hiding. Out of London."

"If he's been banished, then the twins won't want us pretending Simon's missing and call the police. It'll make them angry."

"That's a fair point," Dad said. "If they've told him to stay away, then a police investigation could mean he'll end up dead. The twins might think Simon rang the coppers. A tip-off."

Mum's lower lip trembled. "I just want to know he's safe."

"He'll be safe if we play this smart." Floyd stood. He had to get out of here; the walls were closing in. "I have to go."

He went out into the hallway and pulled on the expensive coat.

Mum had followed him. "You'll let us know, won't you, if you find out he's been banished? I'll sleep better if I know for sure."

"Yeah," he said and forced a smile.

He leaned down and gave her a hug, her body fragile against his.

"See you when I see you, Dad," he called and left the house.

The cold air cut through the emotional fog. He walked quickly, not looking back, his footsteps crisp on the wet pavement. He reached the car, its windows reflecting the grey cloudy sky, and slid into the driver's seat. He pulled out his phone, sending a message to ask if there was time for a quick call. His phone rang seconds after he'd hit SEND. Floyd answered it.

"Yeah?" It sounded like George.

"I need to talk."

"Look, we told you to fuck off home and keep your nose clean. What do you want?"

"My parents. They're asking questions about where Simon is again."

A pause on the other end. "And?"

"I managed to calm them down, for now." Floyd checked the house to make sure Mum wasn't spying through the window. "The

37

narrative ended up that he's been banished, which'll save Mum phoning the police to report him missing."

"Banished. Good one, keep them thinking that. It's safer for you." George hung up.

Stomach rolling, because Floyd knew what George had really meant, he drove away. If he didn't keep the story going of banishment, then he'd likely find himself hanging from the chains in the twins' cellar and being tortured. He'd seen how that had gone down with Simon, and he wasn't prepared to go through it himself.

He'd continue to lie through his teeth.

Chapter Four

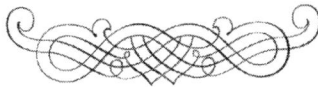

George Wilkes sat with his back to the wall in their pub, the Noodle, not quite hidden but not seeking attention either. His suit, light-grey wool, was a bit tight round the back. After Christmas, he was going on a diet.

Across from him, his twin, Greg, strained the fabric of his own suit, except he'd been using their home gym a lot, something he'd set up in one of the spare bedrooms, and he'd bulked up.

"So, Floyd." Greg took a long pull from his coffee, froth forming a moustache.

"What about him?"

"What about him?" Greg wiped his mouth using a napkin from the cutlery pot in the middle of the table. "He's a potential problem. His *parents* are."

George nodded, his gaze fixed on a condensation ring left by his lager glass on the table. "So, we sort him. Before he becomes a proper problem."

"You did hint you might not be finished with him yet."

"I did. I said I'd go back for him if I got bored."

"And have you?"

"Not yet. For reasons."

"Which are..."

"Simon disappearing off the face of the earth, fair enough. But if Floyd *also* vanishes? Two brothers, gone. That's going to raise eyebrows. It's going to look deliberate."

Greg leaned back. The chair creaked under his weight. "So we leave him, risk letting him put his foot right in it with his mum and dad?"

"No, we don't. We think. We don't just walk in with a sledgehammer, not on this one. Not if we want to avoid a full-blown police investigation, one where they connect the dots. Because you can bet the parents will report Floyd missing. He's their favourite, if you remember. I agree we need to move him off the board, but carefully."

Greg sniffed. "We watch him. Put some feelers out. See what he's really up to. See if there's a better way to make him fuck off."

A shrill, piercing shriek cut through the low background music and chatter. A crash followed, then the sound of a glass shattering. All heads swivelled towards the source. Over by a table occupied by a group of women, two were locked in a struggle. Laura, her face a mask of rage, had Maisie by the hair, yanking her head back. Maisie, smaller but feisty, clawed wildly, trying to land a punch.

"You fucking bitch!" Laura roared. "You think you can take me for a twat?"

"I needed it," Maisie said. "Just for a bit. I'd have paid you back."

The other customers either tried to edge away or were getting closer for a better look.

Greg tutted. "Sodding hell…"

George rose. "This is bad for business, and it's bloody annoying."

Greg pushed himself up as well, his bulk nudging the table and sending George's pint glass over. George set off, cutting a path between the crowd. People made way, eyes widening now the twins were about to get involved.

"Oh, fuck me, there's trouble coming now," someone said.

George extended a hand and clamped it on Laura's arm. Laura tried to pull away and continued scrapping, but he gripped her harder.

"That's enough, love," he said.

Greg took Maisie by the shoulder. The hair she'd been holding in her fist slipped free, and she stumbled back, breathing heavily, her eyes wild with adrenaline.

Laura, panting, her face flushed and streaky with tears, sweat, and running mascara, glared at George. But a flicker of something else appeared in her eyes: recognition and fear now she'd calmed down and seen who'd intervened.

"What's the issue here?" George asked.

Laura pointed a trembling finger at Maisie. A red false nail dangled, clinging to a cuticle, and she picked it off. "She owes me, that's what. Asked for a tenner, promised to pay me back Tuesday. That was a week ago, and now she's asking for more? The nerve!"

Maisie, her hair dishevelled, her clothes rumpled, shrank under Laura's accusation, her eyes red-rimmed and full of shame. "I just... I needed it. For the kids. My Universal Credit hasn't come through, and the gas is going to run out."

"Yet you're in a pub, drinking," Greg said.

Maisie blushed and appealed to Laura. "I swear I'll pay you back. Just not today." She said to George, "I asked her for another tenner, just to tide me over tonight."

"Tide you over with vodka?" Greg asked.

George looked at Maisie. He reached into his jacket pocket and pulled out an envelope. "Take it—go home and put the fucking gas on. And pay Laura back what you owe her." He glanced at Laura. "And that's the end of it, understood?"

Maisie stared at the thick envelope, then at George. "But… I can't…I can't pay all this back."

"Take it," George repeated. "And don't you *ever* make a scene in our pub again."

Tears welled up in Maisie's eyes. "Thank you."

George nodded. "Get your priorities straight. Now fuck off, the pair of you."

He walked back towards their table, Greg falling into step beside him. They sat, George righting his fallen glass, and the customers breathed again. Conversations resumed, but at a lower volume, laced with glances towards them.

"Bloody alley cats," Greg muttered.

George didn't comment. He thought of the envelopes he always carried, which could easily solve a dozen small problems like Laura and Maisie's. But they wouldn't solve the Floyd problem.

The bloke's a ticking bomb.

Rain tapped against the windows, drawing his attention that way. He looked out, the distorted reflections of the pub's interior reflected on the glass. The softness he'd just shown would be a stark contrast to what he'd have to do to Floyd if he didn't keep his mum and dad in check.

44

Christ, some days it just never ended.

Chapter Five

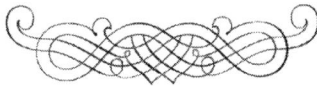

The night Amelia and Brenda stepped into the Dog and Bone wasn't meant to be anything more than a break from a life that had become boring, a neat row of days spent doing her job in Woolworths, going home for dinner, listening to some music, then bed. And then it started all over again the next day. She hadn't seen or heard from Lenny since Malcolm's party and had

stupidly hoped he'd been asking after her, about where she worked, so he could meet her afterwards, but no matter how many times she looked outside the shop as her shift ended, he wasn't there.

She must have read more into it. How stupid of her to have thought he fancied her, just because he'd walked her home and kissed her lips. He'd probably had a right laugh at her expense, telling his friends how she'd fallen for his charm, and oh my God, these ugly girls really did think highly of themselves.

The pub pulsed with easy laughter and multiple conversations, the same as it always did, but Amelia wasn't here for the usual. Like at Malcom's party, she didn't want the 'same'. Brenda had promised something different tonight and, with Amelia sick of pining for Lenny when it was clear he wasn't interested, it was time to move on and try to snag someone else's attention. She wouldn't be silly this time and think that a good-looking bloke wanted her. She'd be content with a plain man like herself. So long as he was nice to her, that was all that mattered.

She saw her wedding in her mind's eye, a scene replayed a thousand times. Not necessarily a grand affair; what mattered was the understanding in the eyes of her future husband. She imagined his hand in hers, a silent promise whispered in the press of skin.

She saw the gentle curve of his smile as she walked down the aisle, a smile just for her.

But the wedding was only the beginning. What she wanted most was the after. The shared quiet of mornings, the way they'd get through the everyday challenges, building a home not just with furniture and paint, but with laughter. She wanted the comfort of knowing someone chose her, every single day, and that she chose him back.

She pictured Sunday mornings with coffee and newspapers, cooking together, maybe burning the toast. Children, tiny hands gripping hers and his, the beautiful chaos of a family she'd helped create.

She shook her head. Maybe she wasn't destined for all that.

But you had the feeling you're going to marry Lenny, remember?

She forced herself to think of something else.

"There's a private room at the back," Brenda had whispered on the phone earlier, when she'd asked if Amelia wanted to go out, "with some...interesting blokes."

Amelia had agreed, anything to break the monochrome monotony, although she did worry that 'interesting' meant boring.

She navigated the crowded space, following Brenda past a row of dartboards on the wall until her friend's ginger beehive bobbed in front of an unmarked door. Brenda pulled her through into the back room. This was new, going in there. She'd heard about it before; people said cards were played there, and you could buy a bottle of booze from behind the bar and drink it in private.

It wasn't grand. A dimly lit bulb hung from a cracked ceiling, and a couple of low-wattage wall lamps gave it a creepy feel. The smoke was even thicker here than in the bar, a haze that softened the edges of everything and obscured the corners. Sofas, sagging and worn, lined two of the walls, their leather shabby on the arms. In the centre, a wooden table littered with glasses, full ashtrays, and a scattering of abandoned playing cards. A wireless perched on a stool by the door, playing 'Shakin' All Over' by Johnny Kidd & the Pirates.

Four men occupied the space. Brenda, now nestled beside one who was as big as a boxer, grinned up at Amelia.

"This is Amelia," she said to them, her arm sweeping.

These men were…different. Definitely interesting but not in the boring way. Sharper, harder around the eyes, with a confidence that bordered on menace. They were the type she usually avoided. They stared at her, not rude but assessing, as if they tried to scrutinise her personality just by looking at her.

One man drew her gaze and held it. He sat at the table. Dark hair, green eyes.

"Evening, Amelia," Lenny said. He pushed a glass of something transparent across the table towards an empty spot. "Have a drink."

She eyed the bottles near him. Gin and another of tonic. She blushed, cursing herself for it. Talk about look naïve and out of her depth. Then she remembered the low lighting and hoped no one had noticed her red cheeks. She sat opposite him and sipped the drink. The gin spread fire on her tongue.

"This lot," Brenda chirped, "are the ones I was telling you about in Woolworths. They're not exactly your usual grafters, are you, Shank?"

Shank, the could-be boxer, smiled, a predatory curve of his lips. "Some of us prefer to choose our own jobs and hours. Keeps life interesting."

Amelia's life was a march of dictated hours. Nine to five, five days a week.

"They like to rebel," Brenda went on.

The most rebellious thing Amelia had done recently was buy a too-short skirt.

The walls seemed to close in on her. She felt under the spotlight, all eyes pointed her way. She drank some more, slurping in her haste and blushed again. God, she wanted to run, just go home and wait for Mum to suggest a neighbour's son for her to date. Finding a man for herself was proving more difficult than she'd thought, especially when she was in the company of handsome lads she had no chance with.

Then, as if a pause button had been pressed to resume play, the conversation flowed, a mix of local gossip, betting tips, and veiled references she couldn't grasp. A lot of things said between Shank and Lenny seemed to be in code. Shank dominated with a quiet authority his friends deferred to, although Lenny challenged him from time to time. Amelia found herself captivated by Lenny, the rhythm of his voice, the way his hands moved, the confidence that seemed to pulse from him.

He asked her about herself, and she told him about Woolies.

"And you find that...fulfilling?" he asked.

She hesitated. "It's a job, even though every day is predictable."

He nodded slowly. "Predictable. Yes, some people like that, but I always find it a bit like watching paint dry."

Was he saying she was boring?

He leaned forward and rested his elbows on the table. "Me? I prefer a slice of danger."

The smoke from Shank's fag swirled around them.

A sting of unease went through Amelia, a delicious shiver that wasn't fear, exactly, but what was it? Once again, she really felt like she didn't belong and should leave. These weren't her type of people, and she wasn't theirs.

"Danger?" she repeated. And now she was sounding like a parrot.

He took another sip of his drink, staring across at her. It was like he challenged her in a game, but she was clueless about the rules.

"Yeah, danger." He licked his lips.

Maybe she could prod him a bit and find out what he meant by that. "What is it you do in 'investments'?"

"What I don't do is stamp papers or balance books. Some might call what I do unsavoury. I prefer to think of it as asset redistribution. From those who have too much, to those who don't. I work when the opportunity strikes, when homes and premises are empty. And sometimes, opportunity has a lock on it and residents are in bed. I'm quiet, and they never know I'm there."

Dread seeped into Amelia's veins, swiftly followed by a surge of excitement.

"Some would say I'm a gangster," he said. "A criminal who enjoys doing robberies, but I see myself as so much more than that. Especially in the future. I've got plans that involve helping every criminal fulfil their potential."

Every criminal? Did that include killers?

The implications were terrifying, dangerous, like he'd said. Reckless. She shouldn't want anything to do with him. He was bad news, Mum would say, and as for Dad… Yet there was something intoxicating about him.

Her life was beige. Lenny's was a violent, vibrant splash of scarlet. Every instinct screamed for her to retreat, make her excuses and go home, get away from these men. But a wilder part of her—the one that would make her more like Brenda—told her life should be lived on a razor's edge.

Was it possible for her to do what Brenda had said and pretend she was confident? The trouble was, she had a feeling that Lenny had already clocked the fact that she lacked self-confidence.

"You…you do robberies," she stated, the words wrong on her tongue because they reinforced that she

shouldn't be talking to him. She heard them, but was she going to listen?

He laughed. "Among other things, love. Nothing too messy, just making sure the scales are balanced, as it were." He smiled, a flash of white teeth in the dim light. "Think of me as a particularly efficient tax collector, only with a bit more persuasive charm than your average civil servant. Or maybe you can think of me as Robin Hood; I take from the rich to give to my poor self, although the way things are going, I won't be poor for long. A man has to have ambition, doesn't he."

She nodded, unsure what to say to that. The other men watched their exchange, nodding in agreement. Brenda had fallen asleep with her head on Shank's shoulder, oblivious. The wireless played on. The music, the smoke, the gin, Lenny's honesty, it all swirled together into a cocktail she shouldn't drink.

Her life, a blanket of muted tones, suddenly had a thread of colour woven through it. She imagined the sterile corridors of the police station if he got arrested, the headlines in the papers, the gossip about him in the streets. Could she stand that? To be associated with that?

She didn't even know why she was asking those questions. It wasn't like he'd asked her to date him or anything. That side of things was firmly in her own head.

"That's quite a profession," she said, for want of something to say—because he'd wanted her to say something, it was obvious by the way he sat there waiting.

"It has its moments," he acknowledged. "Always keeps you on your toes. Never a dull day, I'll tell you that much. So, Amelia, what do you make of it all?"

Her mind raced. This was everything her parents had warned her against. Everything society deemed wrong, reckless, criminal. And yet, she couldn't deny the thrill winding through her. The dull ache of routine had vanished, replaced by a thrumming vitality.

She felt alive.

"It's...different," she hedged. "Very different to what I'm used to."

"Different good, or different bad?" he challenged, his eyebrows raised.

She met his gaze, a spark of boldness lighting up inside her. "Different...exciting."

His smile widened. "Exciting. I like that." He gestured to her empty glass. "Another?"

"Please," she said.

He poured her a generous gin, adding only a splash of tonic.

This drink went down faster than the first. The music swelled, a jazzy number, and the room seemed to tilt. The edges of the conversation blurred. Lenny spoke of risk, of nerve, of living by your wits, and freedom, of not being beholden to anyone. Amelia's head buzzed with the effects of the gin and hearing about this new world.

They talked for what felt like hours, though it could have been only minutes. The smoke grew thicker, her world outside the pub insignificant—she didn't care what her parents were doing, didn't care if she never went back to Woolies ever again. All that mattered was her and Lenny, talking. The conventional upbringing she'd had, the safe choices, the sensible path, she had the urge to throw it all away and run into the life Lenny had painted with his words.

He leaned forward again, his voice dropping. "I think I need to get you home. Your mate's off her face, so Shank will take care of her."

The next thing Amelia registered was the cool night air on her face, a shock after the muggy heat of the back room. She vaguely worried that someone who knew her parents would spot her, go running back to tell tales, but at the same time, what did she care? She was doing what they wanted, finding a husband so she could get out of their hair.

She swayed slightly, but Lenny's hand was firm on her elbow, guiding her up the pavement. The streetlights fuzzed into halos, and the hum of traffic sounded far away. Everything sounded far away. It was like she and Lenny were in a bubble.

She stumbled and almost went flat on her face.

"Easy," he said. "Looks like you've had a proper night of it."

She giggled. "I think I have. That gin, it snuck up on me."

"Don't worry. I'll see you home."

That was the second time he was doing that. It had to be a gentlemanly thing, the way he'd been brought up. He hadn't looked at her in any kind of way in the back room, as if he fancied her, but maybe he liked to play his cards close to his chest. And maybe she'd invented the hand she currently held, hoping to scoop up all the winnings.

She had to remind herself he wasn't interested in her in that way.

That thought and the cold air sobered her slightly, but the world still spun around her. Her thoughts were a jumbled mess of gin and 'Shakin' All Over' and crimson threads and Lenny's dangerous robberies. He didn't try to take advantage of her state, didn't press for anything more than an arm around her waist to *keep her upright. He was a polite gentleman, despite the dark confession he'd made earlier, that he was basically a criminal.*

They walked in silence, the music from the pub fading, replaced by the hushed whispers of the wind through the trees. She stole glances at him. He was a mystery she wanted to unravel. The thrill of his world buzzed in her veins. She knew damn well she wasn't the kind of person who'd fit well there, but he'd made her want to step inside it.

They reached her quiet, respectable street. It looked bland. Boring.

Lenny stopped at her gate. "Here we are."

She fumbled in her bag for her key. She found it and looked up at him, her view still a little unfocused. "Thank you, Lenny."

He smiled down at her, his expression softening the lines around his eyes. "I'll be in touch. Take care."

No kiss this time, then. Maybe he didn't want to take advantage of her because she was drunk. He waited until she'd unlocked her front door, then turned and walked away. Inside, Amelia leaned on the closed door, the cool wood pressing against her cheek. The house was quiet, still, safe. And dull.

Nothing would ever be the same again. She'd had a peek into another dimension. The sensible, predictable Amelia had met the vivid splash of Lenny. The music from the radio, the clinking of glasses, the heady scent of smoke and gin, it all lingered in her mind, a promise of a dramatic, exciting, and perhaps dangerous future ahead of her.

She shouldn't want it.

But she did.

Chapter Six

The rain had been falling all day, a moody curtain that had draped itself over the manor. On the floor of Simon's old study lay a large leather suitcase containing the spoils of a dead man's sins. It used to be kept in a big holdall, but Floyd had moved it to the case, feeling it was safer there and a lot easier to transport. Wheels on suitcases, a genius invention.

Floyd had 'inherited' the money, seeing as Simon was dead. Only he and Floyd knew it existed, so Floyd had no qualms about keeping it for himself. Actually, scrap that, the twins knew. He recalled one of them saying he ought to buy something for his parents out of it, or words to that effect.

He still hadn't. He'd do that soon. A nice bracelet for Mum and a watch for Dad. Enough time had passed since he'd come out of prison that they'd believe he'd been saving up for the gifts.

Floyd's life had been weird since Simon had died. The silence here was deafening, so much so he usually had the radio or telly on for background noise. He hadn't worked for ages, wanting to keep his head down, but the laziness was doing his nut in. He had itchy feet, the urge to do something. Step back into his old world, even though he didn't exactly need to earn money at the minute.

He ran a hand over the cool surface of the suitcase. This money, metaphorically stained with the blood of strangers, was a small fortune.

It could buy him a new life. He'd spent time in prison for murdering a fifteen-year-old girl— he'd been seeing her, thought she was older, and when she'd admitted she wasn't...he'd lost the fucking plot. Since his release, he'd been doing a few odd jobs in the criminal world to keep the wolf from the door, but then Simon had come calling, needing Floyd to dispose of women's bodies.

Jesus, I should have said no.

He needed a distraction, and there was only one place to go for that. He could pick up a job there, get rid of this lethargy.

He hid the suitcase and left the house, driving from rural into urban. He navigated streets that were a distortion of smudged lights and rain-streaked windows. He reached his destination, a 'café' tucked away down a side street. It was a place that didn't advertise; it didn't need to. Its clientele found it via word of mouth. Those with too much to hide met over tea or coffee and whispered deals. Floyd had been a few times with Simon, who'd always seemed so uncomfortable there, as though he wasn't a criminal, yet he was a fucking killer.

Floyd had learned to blend into the shadows while in prison, to listen and not be heard. Now, he'd listen and try to pick up a job.

Inside, he sat at his usual table. Amelia, the annoying old woman who ran the place, shuffled towards the counter to make his coffee. It bothered him that she'd memorised everyone's drinks, yet at the same time he envied the way she could do that.

He watched the comings and goings, earwigged the hushed conversations, spotting the quick glances that passed between tables. He was a wealthy man, but here, in this den of wolves, he was seen as skint. Better that they thought that, although he was surprised that bloke he'd stupidly told about the suitcase hadn't tried to rob him or get someone else to do it.

He should know better than to brag. Simon had been a bragger.

Amelia arrived, placing his drink down, her hand out for the hundred quid she expected. He took some notes out of his wallet and laid them on her palm. She folded them and pushed them up her sleeve.

"Fancy seeing you here, dear," she said. "I haven't seen you since...well, since Simon was around."

Was she fishing? Why, though? As far as she was concerned, Simon didn't come here anymore because she'd told Floyd to tell him he wasn't welcome. Had she heard any whispers? And Amelia had never called him 'dear' before. In fact, she'd always been abrupt with him. Rude. He'd always felt her criticising eyes on him, the creepy cow.

"Simon's stayed away, like you wanted," he said.

She smiled, a papery stretch of her lips that gave him the willies. She lowered to the chair opposite him, her movements agile despite her age.

"Err, was there something you wanted?" Floyd asked.

She smiled again. "Just sitting with one of my favourite customers."

"Favourite?" Suspicion had him on edge.

"Well, you're always the polite one, unlike some of the brats who pass through these doors. I heard Simon always had a way of getting what he wanted."

Her random switch to Simon was well odd. Why was she interested in him?

"Yes," Floyd said, "he could be persuasive."

"I heard he moved out of that manor of his. Must be lonely for you now he's gone, seeing as you'd only just got reacquainted after you got out of the nick." Amelia cocked her head. "Did I hear that you'd moved into his gaff?"

She had to have people telling her gossip. He'd told a couple of people he'd moved in at Grove when he'd been in the pub a while ago.

"Must be strange to be all alone in that massive house," she went on.

"I manage," he said. "It's a big adjustment, keeping all those rooms clean."

"Oh, I'm sure it is, especially when there are bits and bobs all over the place. Some of them quite valuable."

She'd definitely been listening—in here. Floyd's heart hammered. It sounded like she knew about the money, but why refer to it as bits and bobs? Simon had mentioned the cash in here, he remembered that, so maybe Floyd wasn't to blame for opening his mouth after all.

"What kind of bits and bobs?" he challenged.

"Oh." She waved a dismissive hand. "You know how it is. In our line of work, bits and bobs don't just disappear when a man does. They leave so much behind…"

Floyd swallowed hard. "I don't know what you're on about."

She stretched her lips to reveal teeth and gums. "Where's Simon?"

He was going to have to fob her off. "Cheltenham. Gave me the keys to his place and told me to look after it."

Amelia raised an eyebrow. "Bit too much for your tastes, isn't it?" She sighed. "I'd love to live in a house like that. This place, my flat upstairs, well, it's not exactly a retirement home, is it?" She gestured vaguely around the grimy café. "Been thinking of selling up, getting out of the smog. Find somewhere quiet, put my feet up."

Floyd looked at her, surprised. Amelia, retiring? The idea was almost unthinkable. "You, leaving the café?"

"Even old dogs yearn for new tricks," she said. "I've got a bit of cash put by, you know. Haven't spent much on myself. Been looking at property, actually. Something with a bit of space, a bit of class. Simon's place sounds rather grand. Is it?"

If Amelia was in the mood for buying, and Simon's place was what she was looking for, maybe Floyd could play a part here.

"It's proper grand," he said. "High ceilings, big rooms, the lot."

"I bet it is," Amelia said, her voice full of childlike enthusiasm. "Tell you what, while Simon's away, and you're there, would you mind if I had a quick look around? Just for inspiration, you understand. To get a feel for what a proper manor's like. My little nest egg might be enough for something like it, you never know. I could even make Simon an offer, if it really suits. Cash. No banks. A quick deal, if the price is right."

The mention of cash, quick and untraceable, was the hook, and she knew it. How much was she talking? Millions, it would have to be. And where the fuck did she keep that amount of cash?

Floyd smiled. "I suppose Simon wouldn't mind, not if it's a serious enquiry. Just a quick look, though."

"Of course," Amelia said, her eyes glittering. "Just a quick look. I won't touch a thing. Just want to see the layout, the gardens, maybe peer into a few rooms, get a feel for the place. What time would suit you?"

Floyd thought for a moment. "I'm free later. Early evening? Six?"

"Six it is," Amelia confirmed, her expression unreadable. "Just you and me and Shank."

Oh God, that old man Simon hadn't liked.

"Err, you didn't mention Shank until now," Floyd said.

"He's my friend, we go back years. I'd be stupid if I came alone. One, you're a criminal, and two, the manor is in the countryside. You could do anything to me out there."

"I'm not like that!" he protested.

She frowned. "But you're a killer, aren't you?"

"But I wouldn't kill *you*, Jesus."

"I'm sure you wouldn't, but I've just told you I have a lot of cash, and some men wouldn't think twice about murdering me to get it." She got up and drifted towards the counter.

Floyd drank his coffee and, unsettled, got up and left.

Was she fucking him about?

EMMY ELLIS

Amelia smiled, watching him go. She waited until the condensation on the window had completely swallowed his retreating silhouette, then she moved away from the counter. She scanned the room, her gaze landing on a figure in the corner.

Shank.

Amelia walked over and sat opposite him.

Shank didn't look up immediately, but his smile said it all.

"You heard all that, then?" Amelia whispered.

Shank met her gaze. "Buying a manor, eh?"

"I'm not bloody buying it—just buying us a way in."

"So you're retiring."

"I am, but keep it under your hat for now. Just make sure you're here in good time to take me to Grove for six o'clock."

He nodded, getting up to make his own coffee.

A surge of anticipation went through Amelia. She was grabbing this opportunity with both hands. And tonight, opportunity wore the face of a fool named Floyd, who'd inherited a hoard she'd make her own.

Chapter Seven

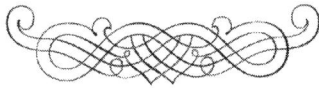

*M*onths had passed since Amelia had met Lenny.
He'd waited for her on the corner of her street
one morning when she went to get the bus for work,
asking her if she'd like to go out with him. He took her
on 'dates' to the Dog and Bone, although it was the
same as that first time there; they sat in the back room
at the table, talking, while Brenda chatted to Shank on

the sofa. It never felt like a proper date, though, no kissing or touching, and it confused her because either he liked her or he didn't. If he didn't fancy her, why did he keep asking her out?

She was meeting him again tonight. She'd got the bus to town and waited for him to turn up. The streetlights cast pools of yellow on the wet pavement that reflected the procession of black cabs and the hurried walk of night-time drinkers.

It was nearly half past seven, and Lenny was late. Again.

Was she that desperate to be with a bloke that she was going to allow this to continue? His lateness, his excuses, his disregard for the fact that she stood there in the rain beneath her umbrella, her feet damp where the wet had seeped inside her shoes. As there was no clear direction of where they were going together, if anywhere, she had to ask herself is she should cut her losses. Yes, they got on well enough, and although Lenny liked the sound of his own voice, she found she enjoyed listening to him. But maybe if another man chatted away to her she'd enjoy that, too. In short, she was trying to work out whether it was Lenny who drew her or was she just fixated on the idea of a relationship—and anyone would do?

She adjusted the strap of her handbag, a worn leather affair. Her newest dress, bottle green, came to her knees and had a full skirt that let the icy air waft up the backs of her legs. Still, standing on this pavement was a far cry from the utilitarian drabness of Woolworths, a place that had become a prison of price tags and polite smiles, so maybe she ought to be grateful that Lenny wanted to see her at all.

A horn blared, and a sleek car, too polished and posh for someone she knew (unless she counted Malcolm), screeched to a halt beside her. The passenger window opened, and she peered inside. Lenny leaned across, smiling.

How on earth did he get a motor like that?

He flashed her a grin. "Sorry I'm late. Ran into a bit of bother."

He always seemed to get into a bit of bother.

The car was a glimpse into a world she'd only read about. She slid onto the seat, the scent of expensive aftershave and leather filling her nostrils.

"Bother?" she asked, trying to sound nonchalant.

Lenny shrugged, pulling away from the kerb. "Just business, love. I tell you what, I've got a place I want to show you. A special place. Thought we'd skip the usual and go somewhere different tonight.

Unique." His smile didn't quite reach his eyes, which remained watchful, scanning the street.

Her vision of tonight's date, which had stupidly involved a romantic setting and Italian fare, something they'd never even done in the past, evaporated. Unique, in Lenny's world, could mean anything. Why wasn't she asking him what he meant? Why did she just let him tell her things without questioning it? Mum had told her never to let a man get the upper hand, even if you gave him the impression he had it, because then they thought they could do whatever they liked, even though they could. It confused Amelia. Either she was supposed to do whatever a husband said or she wasn't.

There were times when it was made really obvious that she wasn't old enough to deal with something like this. Supposed dates with Lenny, being in a relationship. She didn't understand the ways of men and women, what she was meant to do, her role in things.

Lenny drove through a maze of streets, then he pulled up in front of an unassuming building. It looked like it might have been a shop once upon a time, perhaps a café? A couple of other empty buildings stood along the way, although it was obvious they'd previously been houses. Condemned signs told her of their future fate.

She returned her attention to the building he pointed to. The windows were covered in condensation. No sign, no name. The street was quiet, save for the distant rumble of traffic and the cry of a mangy tabby cat who wandered up the pavement.

Lenny turned off the engine. She glanced from the building to him.

"Don't look so nervous," he said. "This place is mine. Well, nearly mine."

"What is it?"

"A café."

They got out, and he led her to the door. He pushed it open, ushering her in. The air was full of moisture and stank of stale fags, coffee, and greasy food. Amelia's eyes adjusted to the dim interior—not all the lights were on. That seemed to have been done on purpose, like the customers wanted gloom to hide in. The room was crammed with tables, each surrounded by a cluster of men. It was a bit grotty, to be perfectly honest, and needed a good scrub. Maybe that's what he wanted her here for, as a cleaner.

One of the men really stared at her. Her initial feeling of unease solidified. These weren't the type of men she saw in the pubs. They sat close, their voices low. Some smoked, the cherry tips of their cigarettes glowing. Others nursed cups of tea or coffee, their gazes sweeping over her with an unnerving vigilance.

Plates of half-eaten sandwiches lay forgotten on some tables, but no one seemed to care. The focus was clearly on the hushed conversations. Maps drawn on bits of notepaper were unfurled, rolls of banknotes exchanged hands. A man with a scar running from his temple to his jawline stared at her for a moment too long, before returning his attention to the cards he held.

This was no café. Not in the way she understood the word.

Lenny moved through the space, a nod here, a word or two there. He gestured to a small table tucked into a corner, surprisingly clean, and pulled out a chair for her. "Make yourself comfortable. I'll get us some tea."

She wasn't sure she wanted to drink from a cup in this place.

He walked behind a counter, leaving Amelia exposed under the occasional, fleeting gaze of the other men. She clutched her handbag on her lap, her pulse thrumming in her temples. Why would Lenny want a place like this? Did he see the potential in doing it up? She did, she could imagine it would shine with a lick *of paint and the condensation wiped from those windows.*

He returned with two steaming mugs of tea. He set one before her, his expression serious, and sat. "Right then, this isn't what you're thinking. Not exactly a date, is it."

She didn't think their evenings in the back room of the pub were dates either, not really, not in the way she'd always imagined dates going. There were no bunches of flowers, no chocolates, no Lenny coming to the front door to collect her. No assurances to her parents that he'd keep her safe.

He must have seen her flinch of disappointment, as he offered an apologetic smile. "Look, I like you. I do."

Her heart lifted.

"But I brought you here for something other than a few drinks and having a chat," he said. "Something…important."

So having a few drinks and a chat with her wasn't *important? Was he really showing her who he was now? Or was he just as crap at dating as she was, and his words were coming out wrong? Just because he was good-looking, didn't mean he knew all the ins and outs of seeing a girl.*

He took a sip of his tea, his gaze sweeping the room again, like it meant more to him than she did. "This place, I rent it from an old geezer who doesn't ask too many questions. Got a long lease. The plan is to buy it outright one day, and the flat upstairs." Fierce determination shone in his eyes, a glint of ambition that momentarily eclipsed the shadow of the criminal underworld that surrounded them.

Because that's what she was sure this was. The underworld.

"What is it, though?" Amelia asked. "Because it isn't a bloody café."

"It's a safe place, love. A meeting point where men can talk strategy, discuss business without fear of prying ears or unwelcome interruptions. The police won't bother us if we're quiet. Discreet." He leaned closer. "Each of these blokes, they pay a fee with every visit, to be allowed to sit here, to talk, to plan, to conduct their affairs. It's exclusive, see? Keeps the riff-raff out. And it keeps the rent paid. And then some."

Amelia's mind reeled. Fee? To discuss illegal activities? This wasn't like the corners of pubs and whatnot, it was a place specifically for criminals to meet, facilitated by Lenny.

He finished with: "All done over a cup of tea and a sarnie."

"So why did I need to see it?"

He leaned back. "The lads, they like their tea. They like their coffee. And they get peckish. Bacon, sausage sarnies. Simple stuff. I need someone trustworthy. Someone who can keep this quiet. Someone who can blend in. Someone who isn't going to run off screaming to the pigs. I've seen you at Woolworths. You're efficient. You're good with people. And you don't gossip."

He's watched me at work?

Even though she'd wanted him to, it didn't seem so romantic now, knowing he'd been at the shop and she hadn't been aware. It felt creepy.

"You're offering me a job?" she asked—could her voice have sounded any flatter?

"Yeah," he confirmed. "Pouring tea. Brewing coffee. Frying up bacon. Keeping the place tidy—but not too clean, we don't want normal people thinking it's okay to come in. I want you here when I'm not. It'll be long hours, late nights. But the pay is more than double what you pull in at Woolworths. Triple once things really get going."

Double, triple her pay? The numbers spun in her head, numbing the moral qualms. She thought of the monotony of her life. This was an escape. A dangerous one, perhaps, but... It was a plunge into the unknown, a leap into a world where rules were rewritten. The thought of earning that much was a heady intoxicant.

She looked around again. The men seemed less menacing now. Lenny was no longer just a date but a gateway. A boss.

Maybe that's all he's supposed to be.

"What do I say to them?" she asked, darting her eyes towards the men to show him who she meant. "If anyone asks."

"You say you're Amelia," Lenny replied. "You work here. That's it. You hear nothing. You see nothing. You remember nothing."

She took a deep breath, the stale, damp air filling her lungs, carrying with it the scent of illicit dealings and the promise of a different future. It wasn't the future she'd envisaged—she flushed now at the idea of being a gangster's bit of skirt—but it was most likely better than nothing. It was a plunge into the unknown, a leap that would alter the course of her life. The reward was freedom from the staid and boring.

"All right," she said. "I'll do it."

Lenny grinned wide. "Good girl. I knew you'd go for it." He stood and held out a hand to help her up. "Start tomorrow. Six in the evening. Don't be late."

As she walked out into the cold night to wait by the car so he could take her home, the lampposts seemed *to glow with a sharper intensity. But that was just fanciful bollocks. The world around her hadn't changed, but her place within it had. She was no longer just Amelia from Woolworths. She was someone else, stepping into the shadows, a teapot in one hand and secrets in the other.*

The weight of her decision settled upon her, but beneath it thrummed a pulse of excitement. It was the thrill of a life less ordinary.

And it was going to be okay.

Chapter Eight

Floyd had unlocked the car and slid into the cold driver's seat outside the café. He'd been sitting there for about ten minutes now, going over his conversation with Amelia. Was this a trick or a setup, or was she really hoping to buy the manor?

He sighed and twisted the key in the ignition. The engine turned over, coughed. He gripped the steering wheel, squeezing it hard to stop himself from gritting out a scream of frustration. He hated not being in control. The image of the way Amelia had assessed him churned his gut.

He pulled away from the kerb and joined the sparse traffic around the corner. He tried to occupy himself with anything but Amelia's visit later, but it wasn't working. It had annoyed him that she'd announced bringing Shank without at least checking if it was okay first. Fuck, what was he doing? He was going to show two old fuckers around his brother's pride and joy, the monument to his ambition and, ultimately, his downfall. Simon, who'd resurfaced in Floyd's life, unexpected and unwelcome, after years of estrangement, expecting him to dump bodies for him.

Now, Floyd was the sole key holder to a multi-million-pound asset, legally unsellable. With Simon only 'missing', the estate couldn't be settled. Not for seven years, he'd read, unless proof of death emerged. That's why Amelia's offer had sparked Floyd's interest. Cash. An untraceable, off-the-books sale. Enough money to disappear, to start over. A new name, a new country, a new life. Freedom.

He took a sharp corner onto a narrower street, leaving the main thoroughfare behind. The houses here were taller, older, their brickwork grimy. The type of house he belonged in. He wasn't Simon. He'd never been driven by greed, by a lust for more *things*. But now, the money Amelia might hand over to him offered safety, away from the twins. But was that greed? Or was it self-preservation?

He pulled up outside his block of flats, a concrete tower from the seventies, its once-white paint now beige. He needed to pick up any mail that had arrived in his absence. He killed the engine and sat in the silence, just needing a minute. His phone buzzed in his pocket, and he flinched, anxiety spiking. He took it out, almost dropping it. It was labelled as suspected spam.

A weird sensation blew over him, like he was being watched. It was probably the twins, or one of their men, as he'd felt like this, more or less, ever since they'd killed Simon. That was why he'd been hiding out at the manor, avoiding going out as much as possible.

Floyd checked his rearview mirror. Nothing. Just his own tired reflection, framed by the back window. But he couldn't shake the feeling. He eyed the parked cars. Had he noticed that black Audi behind him on the way here, a brief flash of chrome and tinted windows, or was it just his paranoia?

Think of the money. Millions. Enough to live out my days in peace.

He opened the car door and got out, sweeping his gaze up and down the street. Someone in a dark coat stood on the corner, seemingly engrossed in their phone. They stood too far away for him to make out any details, but something about their posture, their stillness, had the hairs on Floyd's neck prickling. He hurried towards the entrance of his building, his keys in hand.

Inside his flat, which seemed so cramped now compared to the manor, he shivered at the quiet. He switched on the hallway light and scooped up letters from the mat, sliding them into his coat pocket. A wallop of nausea sent him off balance, and he rushed into the kitchen, running the tap while he found a glass in the cupboard. He drank a full one, then shut off the water.

He walked to the window, drawing back the thin curtain. The figure on the corner was still there, a dark silhouette. It might be nothing. It might be everything. Simon had seen similar from the window of his flat in Cheltenham. The outfit he'd been involved with had sent men after him. Was Floyd's life going to go down the same path? Would he also end up dead?

He thought of the manor, the oppressive weight of it on his shoulders, its dark secrets. And Simon, the brother he'd never got along with yet had helped regardless, the brother who had, even in death, ensnared him in a trap of deceit and danger.

His phone rang again. Another unknown number.

Was it the twins using a new burner?

He felt like the clock was ticking down to something bad.

A decision had to be made. Freedom or conscience?

He had a feeling freedom was going to win.

He was going to leg it.

Chapter Nine

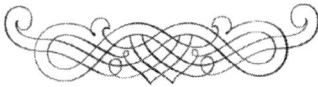

George sat behind the wheel of their little white van. Beside him, Greg scrolled idly through his phone, the screen's blue glow bright in the encroaching dusk. They'd been driving around for a while, checking their usual routes for anyone misbehaving, stopping to chat with those who waved them to the kerb to report anything amiss. Their route was a familiar combination of power and presence, a normal patrol through their Estate. Greg was currently checking in with the other leaders on the WhatsApp group to see if there was anything that needed to be addressed.

"Anything going on?" George asked.

Greg shrugged. "It's nothing we need to worry about, but some Albanian crew are trying to muscle in on the market stalls on Moon's Estate. I'll send a message to ask if he'd like some help, but now that he's got Alien and Brickhouse running the show for him, he's bound to say no."

George dipped into a side road they hadn't been down since the beginning of their time as leaders. They'd established it was of no use to them, the old café there closed up, but the satnav suggested it was a convenient shortcut to get to their destination, Crawshaw Street, and the shops there. They'd show their faces to remind people it was never a good idea to withhold paying them protection money. They usually sent Martin, but going in person every now and then kept the owners on their toes.

He frowned. Lights glowed in the old café. "Hang on a fucking minute…" He slowed the car, nudging the kerb in his haste and coming to a stop.

Greg looked up, phone forgotten, sliding it into his pocket. He followed George's gaze. "What the...?"

The windows were completely obscured by condensation, like frosted glass. George would bet there'd be a big-arse mould problem in there. It was impossible to see inside. The building itself, red brick stained dark with years of London grime, had the remnants of an awning, the metal contraption still there but the fabric long gone.

"No one told us that was open," Greg said.

"Hmm." George narrowed his eyes. If this was a café, a functioning business, the owner should be paying their dues. "No foot traffic, so I'd be surprised if it ever got busy. Let's go in and see what's what."

They got out. George buttoned his new dark-grey coat, one that reached his knees. He pushed the café door open. The warmth hit him immediately—seriously bloody hot humidity, which explained the condensation on the windows. Maybe the place wasn't open for business yet—and it shouldn't be. The décor was worn, Formica tables and mismatched chairs scarred from use.

Conversation died. The customers were all men, and George knew almost every single face. He made eye contact with some, receiving curt nods in return, but others avoided his stare, like they were worried about being caught in here. He looked in the corner. An old woman sat there, as old as the building itself. She raised her eyebrows as they approached, her eyes sharp. There was no fear in them.

George got straight to it. "Who's in charge here?"

The old bird smiled. "Me."

George gave her a tight smile. "If this is a business, it's a new one to us. What exactly is this place?"

She took a slow sip of her tea, her gaze unwavering. "It's apparently polite to introduce yourself to someone new, but I suppose you two don't think you need any introduction. I've no doubt you'll want to know my name. Amelia. And this place is mine. I own it. As for what it is, it's a community hub. For my late husband's friends."

Err… "Do I know you?"

"Never had the pleasure of a face-to-face chat in my life," she said.

Her voice. He'd heard it somewhere before. "Did you happen to ring me recently? Last month?"

"Not me."

George raised his eyebrows. He'd let it go, for now, but if this was the same woman, she'd phoned him about Floyd and Simon. Grassed the pair of them up. "So this gaff. A *community* hub? For all these...friends?" He swung his gaze around, taking a silent inventory of men who'd long left community spirit behind, if they'd ever had it in the first place.

Amelia smiled faintly. "My husband had a lot of friends. From all walks of life, you might say. All sorts of professions."

Greg shifted from foot to foot, clearly getting impatient. "Look, if this is a café, a proper business, then it's being operated on our patch. And we weren't informed. There are protocols." The unspoken threat of protection money hung in the air.

Amelia's gaze settled on Greg. "Protocols, yes. I'm well aware of protocols. But this place is just a gathering point. A place where associates can meet, without fuss, without trouble."

"Who was your husband?" George asked.

Amelia's eyes narrowed. "Lenny Bagby."

The name landed in the silence, sending ripples through George. Lenny Babgy. He'd heard the name, of course, whispered by the old-timers when he was a boy, a legend from the myths of London's underworld.

"So," Amelia continued, "now you know who I am and what this place is, you're welcome to a coffee, if you like. But there's no protection to be paid here. There never will be."

"A coffee? Perhaps another time," George said.

They left and got back in the van.

"Lenny Bagby," George said.

"Bloody hell. I thought he was just some bloke in a story. I never really took all that Robin Hood lark seriously. Mind you, I was never as interested in the gangsters as you were. You were always listening."

George pulled away from the kerb. He glanced in the rearview mirror to catch a glimpse of something, but the condensation had remained on the café windows. "She's his widow. Running a place for his old contacts. A safe house for the old guard—or so she'd like us to believe."

"And all those faces in there," Greg mused. "We had no fucking clue that's where they meet." He laughed.

George didn't. "I don't find it fucking funny that people on our Estate, who are meant to do as they're fucking told, have never once told us about that hub. Hub, my arse." He gripped the steering wheel, pissed off. "We need to look into this. Everything. Who Lenny Bagby was. What he really did. And who else might be still out there, linked to him—and her. Because if that little old woman can bring all those men to heel with nothing but a kettle and a teabag, then there's a hell of a lot more to this."

"Right," Greg said. "Looks like we've got some history to dig up."

They trundled along the streets, the secret of the community hub fading behind them, leaving only questions in George's mind and a gnawing sense of rage that so many people had been keeping it a secret.

Chapter Ten

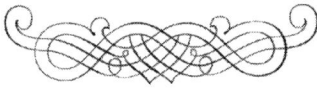

1966

The heavy velvet curtains, a shade of deep red, pulled shut against the afternoon sun, plunged Amelia's new home into a strange twilight. She'd moved out of home and into the flat above the café, much to people's shock. It was as if she'd committed a crime, when all she'd done was grab at the chance for a better life.

But maybe the reactions had something to do with the wedding and the reason for it.

It had been two months since the hurried, quiet affair at the registry office, Amelia's burgeoning belly hidden beneath the loose folds of a cream dress—no white for her, and she wasn't brave enough to overrule her mother there. Now, the dress hung in the wardrobe, a fragile shell of a dream that had shattered just last week.

The silence of the flat had become a suffocating prison since the miscarriage. It echoed her emptiness, a vast, hollow space where a tiny flutter had once been. The doctor had been kind, but he couldn't mend the rip in her soul.

"These things happen, my dear. You're young; there will be other chances."

There wouldn't be. Not for her. The thought of enduring such hope, such pain again, twisted her stomach. She lay on the sofa, the one Lenny had insisted on buying. Its pattern of beige and brown roses and leaves now looked garish, overwhelming. Her gaze was fixed on the ceiling, tracing the faint cracks that spiderwebbed across the surface. Each *fracture seemed to mirror a new fissure in her slowly fragmenting headspace.*

During 'the difficult time', as she thought of it, Lenny had brought her tea, held her hand, tried to play the good husband, just like he'd tried to play the good boyfriend. He never quite hit the spot. And there had been an undercurrent she couldn't name at the time, something that had the hairs on her arms standing on end.

It was two days after the worst of it, when the physical pain had dulled to an ache, the emotional side rawer than ever, that she'd said to him, "I can't go through that again. I don't want to try for another child."

Lenny had been pacing but stopped, his back to her, his shoulders rising and falling with a deep breath. She'd braced herself for an argument, for the firm, unwavering conviction that typically followed any declaration of hers that deviated from his plans. She'd soon realised that he loved to call the shots, she didn't have a say in anything; he'd manoeuvred her into his life and his café, he'd decided when they'd started having sex, even though he hadn't even given her much of an inkling that that was the direction he wanted them to go in. She'd gone along with it all, drifting, accepting.

"I agree," he said.

Amelia blinked. "You...agree?"

He nodded. "This is better." He gestured between them. "Better without any nippers in the way."

The words, perhaps meant to be comforting, had resonated with a peculiar chill. *Better without any nippers in the way.* What was better about it? She was aware now that what he'd said was important and she hadn't given herself any time to dissect it. She'd been too upset about the baby to dig into what her husband had really meant. But as the days had passed, and in a desperate attempt to fill her mind with something other than her heartbreak, she'd started to see it. Or rather, she recognised what she'd unconsciously dismissed for too long.

Lenny always had the last say. Every decision, big or small, eventually circled back to his preference. The colour of the new curtains, the brand of tea, where they went on their rare outings. The clothes she chose, the amount of makeup she should put on—none at all, according to him, especially when she was in the company of the men in the café. Bit by bit, he'd introduced more rules, ones he expected her to obey.

He'd present options, often swaying her towards his choice, then finally nod, accepting her supposed decision with a benevolent air, as if she'd chosen the *correct conclusion without his influence. And if she ever dug her heels in, resisted, he deployed logic, cajolery, and just enough wounded silence to make her feel unreasonable. Or selfish. Or wrong. Eventually, she conceded, and he'd smile, a victor without ever needing to raise his voice.*

He got his own way. Always.

She'd known it was going on but had chosen not to see it. She was excited, having got what she wanted, a husband and a baby on the way, a lovely flat he'd done up for her, and a job downstairs on her doorstep, which she could do still do with the baby, although she wasn't sure she'd wanted it to sit in its pram with all that fag smoke around.

But that wasn't how things had turned out. She still had the husband and the flat and the job, but she no longer had the desire to do what had to be done to maintain it all. The flat, once a symbol of their future, now felt like a cage. Every piece of furniture reflected his taste, his choices. She'd tried to assert herself with the kitchen wallpaper, wanting a sunny yellow, but he'd steered her towards green.

"You'll thank me for it in the long run," he'd said. "Yellow would have got grubby quick."

Now, as she lay on the hideous sofa, she understood exactly what had happened. She'd been blinded by the suddenness of her pregnancy, the societal pressure to legitimise it, so much so that she hadn't really seen who he was at all. Was Lenny the protective man she thought she'd married or someone far more insidious, a manipulator cloaked in charm and concern?

Brenda, the evenings out with her, Amelia's independent trips to town, they'd all diminished to nothing.

"Why go out with her when you've got me?" he'd murmured, his hand tracing the line of her jaw.

The miscarriage had stripped away layers of naivety, leaving her raw and exposed, but also wide awake. The obscuring fog was lifting, revealing a landscape she barely recognised. Subtle control, unspoken demands, a life being lived entirely on his terms.

A click of the front door, then the steady thud of his heavy boots on the polished floorboards announced his return. She didn't move, didn't have the energy.

He paused in the doorway of the living room, his silhouette filling the space. "Still lying there, darling? You should eat something."

She saw this as a practiced performance now, not him showing concern. What he was really saying was *she'd wallowed on the sofa for far too long and his dinner wasn't ready.*

She pushed herself up, her limbs stiff. "I'm not hungry."

He sighed. "You look peaky. Your eyes are red."

Meaning, she didn't meet his standard.

"I've been crying," she stated flatly, unwilling to add any apology or explanation.

He knelt beside the sofa, reaching for her hand. "Life goes on, and we have each other." He squeezed her hand. "Do you remember what I said? Better this way. More time for us."

The words twisted her gut. He'd moulded her grief into an affirmation of his own desires. The more time for 'us' didn't really exist. She barely saw him.

"I need to go out for a while." He got back to his feet. "Some business I forgot I need to attend to. Shouldn't be too long."

Amelia's head snapped up. "But you've only just got back."

He offered her a smile, but his eyes held a glint of something unyielding. "It's important, can't be helped."

She wanted to scream, to rail against his casual dismissal of her pain, his constant need to be elsewhere, his secret life that she was never privy to. But the words died in her throat, choked by the fear that tiptoed into her heart. What if she was wrong? What if she was just being hysterical, as he sometimes implied, and she *was the one with the issue?*

Her attention moved to what he'd taken out from under his jacket. A gun, its steel glinting faintly in the dim light coming from the lamp. She'd seen it before, briefly, when he'd opened a drawer in their bedroom.

He was going out on a proper criminal job.

Or he'd revealed the gun as a warning to her? Do as you're told or I'll shoot?

He slipped it back into an inner pocket. Adjusted his tie, a small smile stretching his lips. He leaned in to kiss her, but she turned her head, offering him her cheek. He kissed it, the pressure of his lips brief and cold. She closed her eyes, listened to the soft clink of his keys, the rustle of his coat, the click of the latch, and then the thud of the front door closing.

He was gone.

The silence was now louder, more suffocating than ever. It crept in on her from all sides. The tears came then, a fresh wave of grief that wasn't just for the child she'd lost, but for the life she'd walked into, thinking it would be exciting. She curled into a ball on the sofa, clutching her empty womb.

The image of the gun burned behind her eyelids.

She'd made a mistake marrying him. A terrible mistake. And now, alone in the trap he'd built for her, she wondered if there was any way out.

The flat was no longer a home. It was a prison, and she was an inmate.

***

The rumble of a passing bus vibrated through Amelia's black shoes, a familiar tremor in the twilight chill of the East End. Evening had drawn a charcoal smear across the sky. A damp, earthy scent mingled with the aroma of burning coal and smoke from chimneys. Leaves, crisp underfoot, skittered across the pavement, as lost and chaotic as her thoughts.

She clutched her handbag tighter. Each step filled her with dread. She hadn't wanted to come, not really. Her mother, Evelyn, rarely offered comfort, preferring instead to dispense practical advice, sharp as a tailor's shears. But desperation slunk in, tight and throttling, and she needed...something. A witness to her unfolding destruction? Someone to tell her she wasn't imagining this...this shitty life she led?

Her happiness had been extinguished. The pram, bought with such hopeful anticipation, stood empty in the spare room, a reminder of what could have been.

Her grief was a private, cavernous space she shared with no one. Certainly not with Lenny. He'd changed, evolving into someone colder—or was that who he'd always been? He was home much less, the hours by herself growing longer, his explanations vague, his eyes, when they met hers, guarded. The easy chatter from the beginning had gone, replaced by a tense quiet that hummed with unspoken things.

Her grief annoyed him.

He'd started smoking again, a habit he'd magnanimously given up when they'd thought they were expanding their family. The stale scent clung to his suits, mingled with a new, unfamiliar aftershave— or was that another woman's perfume? There were phone calls, short and hushed, always in the hall, always when she was just out of earshot. He'd scowl if she came too close. And the money. He was spending more. New shirts, expensive ties, the watch flashing on his wrist a beacon of a secret life without her in it.

Amelia turned a corner, the streetlights casting long, dancing shadows onto the wet brickwork of the terraced houses. The street of her childhood. It hadn't changed since she'd left it, and why would it? She hadn't been gone long, but God, it felt like a lifetime. The front door, painted the same green, the garden wall with its missing brick. She hesitated with her hand hovering over the brass knocker. What was she even going to say? "Mum, I'm broken in a way that scares me…"

She knocked, a tentative tap that felt too small for the enormity of her problems. She should be battering that door. Footsteps approached, Mum opened up. Her expression conveyed mild surprise rather than welcome.

"Amelia. Goodness. I didn't know you were coming." As expected, Mum's clipped voice held no warmth.

"I didn't realise I needed to make an appointment."

"Got a mouth on you now you're married, have you?" Mum raised her eyebrows.

"Sorry. I just needed to talk."

Mum stepped aside, leaving just enough room for Amelia to slip past. The hallway smelled of beeswax polish and the wood of furniture that had occupied the same spots for years.

"Lenny isn't with you, then?" Mum closed the door.

"No. He's working late."

"Always working, that man. Good for him. A man needs to provide." Mum led the way into the sitting room.

Crocheted antimacassars protected the arms of chairs, and every surface held an ornament. A standard lamp illuminated the floral carpet. Amelia wished she still lived here, amongst all the cluttered crap.

"If you want a cuppa, you know where the kettle is." Mum settled into her favourite armchair, her back ramrod straight. "How's it been?"

Amelia perched on the edge of the sofa. "Hard. Since the baby."

A tut escaped Mum's lips. "These things happen. Nature's way. Best not to dwell. You're young, you'll have others. Plenty of time."

She said all that as if she'd rehearsed it, ready for when Amelia visited.

"But I do dwell," Amelia whispered, her voice choked. "I can't help it. And Lenny…he's not the same. He's changed. Or maybe I had rose-coloured glasses on and didn't see him for who he really was."

Mum sighed, a sound of irritation. "Men do change. What did you expect, a lifetime of gazing into each other's eyes like lovesick fools?"

"No, it's more than that. He's distant. He's always out or on the phone, whispering. He's not himself." Amelia twisted her hands in her lap, the words tumbling out now. Was she that desperate to be heard that she'd chosen her mother, of all people, to offload to?

She should have gone to see Brenda, but she might not want to talk to her now because she hadn't been in touch for ages. Brenda wasn't seeing Shank anymore either, so it wasn't like they could get together for a foursome date.

"I think he's hiding something," Amelia said.

Mum's gaze sharpened, something like interest in her eyes. Was this a juicy bit of gossip for her? Her own daughter's upset was cause to get excited? Would she advance on Dad as soon as he got home from work to tell him what was said? "What do you mean?"

"I don't know. He's preoccupied. Secretive. I found a receipt the other day in his coat pocket. For a restaurant I've never heard of, in a part of town we never go to. Two meals."

Amelia's voice cracked. The suspicion, an ache just beneath her grief, had grown into a sharp, piercing pain. Infidelity. It was the most obvious conclusion, yet it felt too simple for the depth of Lenny's transformation. There was a conniving edge to him now, a watchfulness, and that worried her more than the thought of another woman. Maybe he'd taken a gangster out to dinner. A proper gangster. Maybe he'd got in too deep and that's why he always whispered whenever he was on the phone. There were so many bad men who visited the café. He could have got himself into trouble with any of them.

"A restaurant receipt," Mum repeated. "And you immediately jumped to conclusions. Men have business meetings, Amelia. They do things that their wives don't know about. You're being melodramatic. Your nerves are frayed from...from the unpleasantness. You need to pull yourself together."

So a miscarriage was unpleasantness?

"But he barely touches me, never has." A tear escaped, tracing a hot path down Amelia's cheek.

"Maybe he hasn't got a high sex drive." Mum watched her. "Men are not built for sentimentality. They're built for providing, for protecting. And sometimes, for straying. It's the way of the world. You're a married woman, and now you understand the realities of it."

Amelia shook her head. "But what if it's more than straying? He's been out so late, some nights not coming home at all. And he's evasive. He snaps at me if I ask too many questions. He's up to something, I know it."

Why was she only now revealing to her mother what she'd known from the start? That he was a fucking bastard? What had she expected, that Mum *would actually be a decent parent and help her run away? Hide?*

Mum leaned forward, her hands clasped. "Up to something? Are you suggesting he's involved in something unsavoury?"

"I just know he's not the man I married. I'm scared of what he's doing. Of what this means for us." Amelia looked at her mother. She needed reassurance, a sign that she wasn't going mad, that her fears were valid. She needed Mum to tell her everything would be all right.

Mum held her gaze, her expression unreadable for a long moment. The silence in the room stretched, taut and nasty. Amelia held her breath, waiting for a word of comfort she knew wouldn't come.

Mum let out a slow sigh. Her lips thinned. "Well, there you have it. Your answer. You wanted the whole shebang. The marriage, the husband, the life you imagined for yourself. You pursued it with every ounce of your stubborn will, despite my reservations about him." A ghost of a past argument, long forgotten by Amelia, stood in the corner. "You made your bed, and now you must enjoy sleeping in the sheets."

The words struck Amelia hard. They weren't advice or even an accusation. They were a pronouncement, a judgment, an 'I told you so'. There was no understanding to be found here.

Amelia stared at her. Mum saw her as a problem to be solved, a mistake to be acknowledged, not a daughter in pain. The grief for her baby, the fear for her husband, the uncertainty of her future, all of it was her own making, her own burden to carry.

Alone.

She stood, her legs unsteady. "I…I should go."

Mum offered no protest. "Yes, well. It's late. Lenny will be wondering where you are. Though I suppose he's too busy to notice, given what you said."

Amelia walked out of the sitting room, through the hallway, and opened the front door. The cool air hit her face, a welcome shock after the stifling atmosphere of the house. She stepped onto the pavement, the door closing behind her. The streetlights seemed dimmer now, the shadows longer, more menacing. Mum's cruel words reverberated in her mind, a mocking refrain: "You made your bed, and now you must enjoy sleeping in the sheets."

She'd known she wasn't going to get comfort, but she hadn't expected to be handed a mirror which reflected only her own culpability, her own choices, and a future she now had to face by herself.

She sighed. She was walking towards home, towards Lenny, towards whatever dark secrets he harboured. The silence of the empty nursery, the coldness of her husband, the unyielding judgment of her mother, all converged into a single certainty. Her bed was made, indeed, and she was about to discover just how cold the sheets truly were.

The tragic sleep had only just begun.

Chapter Eleven

When those two figures had filled the doorway, Amelia had experienced a frisson of nervousness. Identical in their stocky build, sharp suits, and the unnerving glint in their eyes, The Brothers had surveyed her domain with an insolent curiosity that she'd instantly recognised as trouble.

The Wilkes twins weren't supposed to have got wind of the café. She couldn't trust that they wouldn't change the dynamics if she allowed them to chat here. They were new money, old violence, a mix she rarely saw these days.

She wiped down the counter, staring at some scrote who'd got up from his table and approached. "What are you looking at?" she barked.

Riley Smith pinched his chin. "The twins have heard about this place, then. Whoops. What was it you told me? A proper little hideaway, where the big boys come to play. 'You'll be safe here,' you said." His gaze lingered on a table where two men were discussing the logistics of a lorry full of electronics they were going to rob. "But they'll be back now, you wait and see." He raised his voice. "None of us are safe."

The little fucker was trying to get everyone to revolt against her.

She glared at him. "You come up to my counter, acting the big I Am, yet your mother's not long stopped wiping your arse for you."

Laughs went round.

She continued. "If I were you, I wouldn't poke my nose in other people's business."

His lip curled. "Right. Well, I'm in the business of poking my nose in, see. I pay good money to sit in here, and if my jobs are compromised now…"

The unspoken threat hung there.

Hot anger rose. Amelia shook her head at him. "My café, my rules, my fees. If you don't like it now that we've got those two sniffing round…*fuck off*!"

Riley chuckled, although she'd definitely surprised him by shouting. "Don't insult our intelligence, love. We all know this place is fucked now *they* know about it."

Amelia's gaze darted to the clock on the wall. Not long until the biggest score of her life. And this prick was threatening…what? To turn her world upside down?

"You don't look like my cup of tea anymore," she said.

Riley's eyes hardened. "Is that your way of saying I'm no longer welcome?" He laughed. "I've paid my money for today, so I'll be back later, but after that, you can stick you manky café up your wrinkly arse."

He strode out.

The others resumed their conversations—she'd bet the main topic was whether they all needed to find a new, safe place to chat. The ease had gone out of the room. They'd felt it, too, the shift in the balance of power, the tremor of a new threat, not only from the twins but Riley.

She spent a while sitting at her corner table, her mind a furious vortex of calculations. The café was mostly empty now, only a few hardcore regulars lingering.

"I'm shutting up for the day," she announced, even though it was early afternoon. "Got shit to do."

Everyone left, and she locked the door. She breathed a sigh of relief, then her phone bleeped. She frowned at the screen. Shank had sent a message. Bloody hell, was he going to cancel on her? She read it, confused by his request, but nonetheless, she'd do what he'd asked.

First, though, she had something to do. She went into the office with its stacks of boxes and ferreted in one for a brand-new burner, one of many she'd bought to sell on to the customers if they needed one. She dialled a number she'd kept memorised. It rang five times, then Charlie answered.

"Yeah?"

"It's Amelia. I need a favour."

A pause. "Amelia? Blimey, you still alive?" He laughed. "Joking. What's the problem?"

"The twins. They've come round my place. Mentioning protection payments. I can't have them near here tonight."

Another pause, then a low whistle. "The twins, eh? What have you got planned for tonight?"

"It's a private matter, and I don't want them seeing me go out or come back. I need them occupied for about six hours, starting from ten minutes ago."

Charlie chuckled. "Six hours of twin-free time. That'll cost you." He was a fixer, a cleaner, a man who offered discreet services to those in the know.

"I'll pay. Double your usual rate. In cash. I'll leave it in my yard behind the wheelie bins."

"Deal. I'll make a few calls. It won't be easy keeping those two busy for that long. Where do you want them diverted?"

"Anywhere but here. Make up some rumour of a stash house, or prostitutes, anything. The farther away from my café, the better."

"Consider it done. But be careful. The twins, they don't forget. If they know it's you behind them being sent on a wild goose chase…"

"Yes, I know." She hung up.

A deliberate smokescreen. It wouldn't solve the long-term problem of the twins, but it would buy her the critical window she needed.

She went up to her flat and collected Charlie's money, going into the yard to hide it. Then she put on her coat and went out the front, checking the street for people who shouldn't be there. Spies. No one appeared to be around, but that didn't mean they weren't. She secured the café door, slipping the key into her pocket along with a set of lock-picking tools, a torch, and a pair of leather gloves.

Despite the worry of the unwelcome visit, her mind was focused. She walked at a brisk pace, the chilly air invigorating her, her path taking her away from the familiar café and towards the darker, more industrial edges of the Estate. She considered what Shank had requested of her; maybe she should keep checking behind to make sure no one was following. She doubted very much that he'd appreciate the twins turning up to their meeting.

She glanced over her shoulder, but no one was there. As it wasn't dark yet, it was much easier to see the doorways and alleys. If the twins had sent someone to follow her, then they were bloody good at hiding.

The warehouse Shank had told her to go had corrugated iron sides that had rusted, the windows long since smashed. A single service road led to it, overgrown with weeds, ending in an isolated parking area.

She'd arrived a little before the agreed meeting time, but so had Shank. He sat in a dark hatchback, likely stolen. He got out, walking towards her.

Then she spotted it. Another car. Also dark. Her heart leaped. She didn't bloody like this. "What's going on? Whose is that?"

"You're not the only one who wanted one last job," Shank said. "I've got some money of my own to collect."

"Where?"

"In there." He gestured to the warehouse.

"Fuck's *sake*!" she hissed. In his message, he hadn't said anything about meeting with anyone else, just that she should go to the warehouse.

"If he goes for me, whack him one." Shank handed her a heavy iron pole.

She put on her gloves then took the weapon, like this was *normal*. She should be questioning this, asking why he couldn't whack whoever it was himself, but maybe he'd be busy elsewhere. She didn't like not knowing what she was walking into, but it wasn't like she could stand here and go through the plan with him when he clearly wanted her to get a move on.

He led the way inside, and she glanced around quickly. Someone loomed at them from the left, and she swallowed down a scream. Her movements and reactions were swift, though. She lifted the pipe and then brought it down on the person's head, hard. She recognised him as the lad Floyd had talked to about his stash of money. Preston someone or other. He cried out, sagged, and fell to the floor. He wasn't out cold, but he was disorientated enough that she didn't think he posed a threat.

Shank grabbed a black briefcase off him and held it down by his side.

"My...my money..." Preston slurred, reaching for it.

"Not anymore," Shank said.

As Preston pushed himself up, Amelia slammed the pole against his jaw. A sickening crunch followed. He went down properly this time, out cold.

The whole thing couldn't have taken more than two minutes.

"What do you want me to do with this?" She held up the pole.

Shank took it off her and went over to Preston. He battered his head and face with a few savage swipes, then dropped the pole on the floor. "That little bastard tried to double-cross me last week."

"What did he think was going to happen here?"

"That someone would be bringing drugs, which is why he bought the money."

"Assuming he really put money in the briefcase..."

Shank knelt and placed the case on the floor, opening it. At least one hundred thousand pounds lay inside. He snapped the lid shut, and they walked towards the exit; she'd be having a word with Shank on the way to the manor. This was not the type of thrill she'd been hankering for, and a bit more of a heads-up would have been appreciated.

A phone rang.

Amelia turned. Preston's pocket had lit up.

"Leave it," Shank said.

They stepped outside.

A voice, close, cut through the air. "Well, well, well. Look what we have here."

Amelia froze. Standing in their path, blocking it, stood Riley.

"What are you doing here?" she demanded. "Following me?"

"Err, no, love, Shank asked me to come."

She whipped her gaze to her old friend. "What?"

Shank's smile looked creepy. "I heard he disrespected you in the café earlier."

The gunshot ripped through the afternoon.

Chapter Twelve

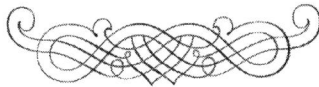

They'd been waiting for nearly an hour, tucked into the shadowed alcove of a disused doorway across the street. George had received an interesting phone call from one of their snouts called Charlie who'd informed them that Amelia wanted George and Greg off her radar tonight. Charlie had already collected the payment from behind a wheelie bin in her yard, something he deserved to keep because he'd been loyal to the twins. George had asked if Charlie knew about the café and what went on there, but the bloke had sounded genuinely confused.

"So how do you know Amelia then?" George had asked.

"My great-granddad knew her husband."

"Right, and she just happened to have your phone number, did she?"

"Yeah, because she babysat me once when I was about ten. She came to my granddad's pub and sat with me—you know my story, Mum and Dad in the nick, my granddad and great-granddad looking after me instead. Anyway, she gave me her phone number and told me if I ever needed any help then I could ring her. She asks me for gossip every now and again, like who's doing what and whether I've heard any whispers. I have to say that today's favour was a more than a little interesting. So what's this about a café?"

"She says it's a community hub for her late husband's friends to sit and have a chat."

"Shame I can't ask my granddads about it. They're both bloody dead."

"Not to worry. Thanks for getting hold of us. Much appreciated."

George had chosen to believe that Charlie was on the level.

The café appeared to be closed. Maybe their earlier visit had spooked Amelia and she'd thought it best to shut up shop.

Then the door opened. A man, the brick-shithouse type, emerged in a black outfit. Shank, some old boy George had seen in the pubs when he'd been a lad watching Ron Cardigan and his cronies as if they were the bee's knees. Shank glanced left, then right. He didn't seem to notice the twins, or if he had he made a good show of pretending not to. He strode towards a bit of a battered car, its paintwork dull and scratched—the possibility of it being stolen seemed high and added to the intrigue about Amelia contacting Charlie and why.

He got inside, and the engine spluttered to life.

In the approaching darkness, George and Greg slipped out of the doorway to their own vehicle, a nicked Mercedes, its tinted windows giving them anonymity. Greg was behind the wheel within seconds. He eased the car along, leaving a safe distance between them and Shank.

The old man drove slowly. The twins followed.

"He's not going home," George said, having got all the information they needed about Shank from Bea, their hacker.

Shank turned onto a familiar road. He parked outside the Noodle. Greg did the same, but much farther away. Shank got out and paused for a moment, scanning the area, then he pushed open the pub door and disappeared inside.

George and Greg waited for a couple of minutes then went after him. Nessa, their manager, polished glasses behind the bar. Her gaze immediately settled on the twins as they walked in. She straightened up, a question in her eyes.

"Nessa," George said. "We've got a question for you."

She nodded, putting the glass and cloth down. "What's up?"

"That old geezer who just walked in." Greg jerked his head towards a quiet corner where the old man sat drinking bitter. "You seen him before?"

Nessa's forehead furrowed. "Him? No."

George exchanged glances with Greg. Nessa wouldn't lie to them. Her honesty was one of her most valued traits. If Shank wasn't a regular, why was he in their pub? Had Amelia told him about their visit to the café, so he'd come here to what, prove a point? That he could encroach on their turf, too?

They walked towards the corner. The handful of drinkers barely registered them, accustomed to George and Greg's quiet authority. As they approached, the old man, still hunched, seemed to sense their presence. Shank lifted his head, his eyes meeting George's.

"Mind if we join you?" George asked. Without waiting for an answer, he sat opposite him.

Greg took the seat beside him, effectively boxing him in.

Shank's grip tightened on his glass, but that was the only outward sign that they'd ruffled his feathers. "I'm just having a quiet drink, fellas."

"Hmm," Greg said. "We've got a few questions."

Shank shrugged. "Fire away."

"We were wondering about a man named Lenny," George began, watching him. "Lenny Babgy, who was married to Amelia. She owns that café, or should I be calling it a community hub?"

A visible tremor ran through Shank, his attention fixed on the condensation on his pint glass. Seemed he didn't want to say anything, though.

"You know them, do you?" Greg pressed. "Lenny. Amelia. You've been to the café, we know that much."

"No. No, I don't know them. Never heard of a Lenny or an Amelia. Just stopped in the café for a coffee, then thought I'd give this place a try."

"Did you hear that, Greg?" George said, not taking his eyes off the old man. "He doesn't know them. Doesn't know a thing. Only went to the café—that we've been told *isn't* a café—for a coffee."

Greg grunted. "Right. He's just a random old fella who decided to drive across half of our Estate to our pub for a quiet pint, after visiting a café run by a woman who we think is lying to us. Okay, mate, we're not going to push you for now, but we'll be in touch."

They got up and walked to the bar. George took his phone out, snapped a discreet picture of Shank, and uploaded it into a WhatsApp chat, adding a caption.

GG: GOT A JOB FOR YOU. OLD MAN, BLACK JACKET, CURRENTLY IN THE NOODLE. I WANT YOU ON HIM FOR THE REST OF THE DAY.

MOODY: GOT IT.

George slipped the phone back into his pocket. He looked at Shank, who stared into his pint.

"Enjoy your drink," Greg called to him.

As they walked towards the exit, George nodded to himself. He had a feeling this was only the beginning of an ugly friendship.

Chapter Thirteen

1967

The evening wind exhaled a damp breath that clung to Amelia's coat as she stepped from their flat onto the pavement. The months had passed, and the air still held the chilly memory of winter. Above, the streetlights buzzed, throwing a jaundiced glow on the grime of the café's brickwork.

"Are you even coming?" Lenny's voice drifted to her from a few paces ahead.

He had Shank at his side, both men already in motion, their shoulders squared, their strides purposeful. Lenny, in his crisp shirt and tightly knotted tie, always looked like he had somewhere important to be, even if it was just the local pub.

Amelia hurried to catch up, the click of her heels tinny compared to the men's heavier footsteps. Her outfit, a dress with a large collar, felt stupid now, too much just to go to the local boozer, but she hadn't been out in such a long time, so she'd got dolled up. They were heading for the Dog and Bone. Lenny had insisted she come along.

"A bit of an outing, eh, love? Liven you up." He'd squeezed her arm, a gesture that was meant to look affectionate but felt like possession.

His reference to her livening up was his way of saying her grief ought to be over by now. Tonight was the end of it, a start of a new phase in their lives.

If only it were that easy.

Inside the pub, the warmth was immediate and stifling. The din of voices, the clatter, the pungent smell of spilled beer and cigarette smoke enveloped her, all a bit much since she'd been keeping herself sequestered in the flat as much as possible and away from the café customers once she'd served their drinks and food. She didn't engage in conversation with anyone unless she could help it.

Lenny, with Shank behind him, navigated the crowded floor to a table tucked away in a corner. So they weren't going into the back room? Blimey, he really did want to liven her up.

Amelia sat with Shank, but they didn't speak while Lenny went to the bar and returned with two pints and a gin and tonic balanced on a tray. She couldn't work Shank out. He never gave much of himself away and didn't seem to feel it necessary to talk to her if he didn't want to. It didn't matter whether it was the polite thing to do. She didn't bother initiating conversation with him either. She suspected it would be wrong, according to Lenny's rules.

"Cheers, everyone." Shank raised his glass.

He was all sharp edges, perpetually on the lookout for something, though Amelia had never figured out what. Trouble? He was a friend of Lenny's from his younger days, the kind of friend who brought with him an unspoken tension. Amelia had always found him unsettling yet alluring.

"Have you seen Brenda lately?" she asked him.

"Not for months."

Lenny frowned. "What do you want to know about her for? She's a little tart who wants to do nothing but get drunk. Anyway, she's gone off with that Malcolm. Got married. He's left his poor person's house and taken her off to his big one in the country. She had a baby last week. Little girl."

Lenny smirked. The bastard was pleased he'd hurt her with that news.

Brenda had got the life Amelia had always wanted.

Brenda had a baby.

The initial hours passed in a haze of alcohol. Lenny was in fine form, regaling Shank with stories, his voice growing louder with each pint. Amelia contributed little, mostly nodding, offering polite smiles. The gin was strong, her head fuzzy, her thoughts slow. She found herself watching the play of light on Lenny's face, the way his dark hair fell over his forehead when he leaned in to share a conspiratorial whisper with Shank.

She realised she didn't much like him.

Shank drank steadily. He kept glancing at Amelia, a look she couldn't decipher. Pity? Or something else?

"Right then." Lenny pushed his chair back with a scrape that turned several heads. "Come on, time we headed off. Got an early start tomorrow."

Amelia breathed a silent sigh of relief. The thought of her warm bed and the quiet of their flat was appealing. She stood, unsteady on her feet, the world swaying gently around her.

Outside, Shank walked ahead. Lenny linked her arm through his, a gesture that used to give her butterflies, but tonight it felt…different. His grip was tight, controlling.

"We're going for a wander," he said, not quite looking at her. "There's a shortcut, through the backstreets. Quieter than the main road."

Amelia hesitated. "It's getting late, and I'm a bit tired."

"Bollocks." He squeezed her arm against his side so that if she wanted to run away she couldn't. "Fresh air'll do you good. Besides, Shank's coming along. We wouldn't want to leave him in the dark alone, would we?"

He exchanged a quick, almost imperceptible glance with Shank who'd looked over his shoulder at them.

What was going on? Something was definitely off. A flash of panic stirred in Amelia's stomach. A shortcut, a new route, in the dark, with Shank. Not that she thought Shank would harm her. Yes, he watched her a lot, which was likely to keep an eye on her for Lenny. Still, her instincts screamed at her, but

Lenny's grip grew firmer, his plastic smile unwavering. To protest further would be seen as creating a scene. She'd learned, over time, that it was easier to acquiesce to his wishes. So, she kept silent, allowing herself to be steered away from the familiar thoroughfare, into the alleys that snaked behind the main streets.

The character of London shifted dramatically here. The vibrant, boisterous sounds of the commercial roads faded, replaced by the hushed whisper of the wind through narrow passages, the distant rumble of a train, and the scurrying of unseen creatures. The streetlights were few and far between, and the buildings were older, soot-stained, their windows dark and blank.

Amelia's unease intensified with every turn. Lenny and Shank had fallen into a low, murmured conversation in front of her, their voices barely audible. They moved with a hurried stealth, their heads bent close. Amelia tried to listen, but their words were indistinct: "...the back...alley...no one... Eleven-thirty..."

She stumbled slightly, her high heel catching on an uneven flagstone. Lenny turned and steadied her.

"Careful, love," he murmured, his focus clearly elsewhere.

They rounded a corner, and the street widened into a small, deserted square. Across from them, bathed in the glow of a single streetlamp, stood a shop. A jeweller's. The pieces clicked into place. The detour. The hushed conversation. Shank's presence. Lenny's strange energy. They hadn't brought her out tonight to liven her up, they'd brought her to case a fucking job.

She stopped dead. "Lenny...what is this?"

He stared at her, his face stripped of all kindness. "Listen, not a word. You're going to wait here, by the corner. Just keep an eye out. If anyone comes, you cough. Two short ones."

Shank stepped forward. "Don't mess this up."

Her mind reeled. A robbery. Lenny expecting her to be involved.

"No. I can't. Lenny, please..."

He gripped her arm tight, digging his fingers into her flesh. "You will, Amelia. Or do you want me to explain to your parents why you were here with us? Do you want me to tell them you're the robber?"

The implication was clear: she was complicit, whether she liked it or not. Trapped.

He pushed her towards the designated spot, a shadowed alcove beside an old newspaper stand. "Just watch. We'll be quick. Ten minutes, tops."

Then, they were gone. They melted into the deeper shadows, moving with an unnerving stealth towards the side of the jeweller's shop, where an alleyway ran.

The cold seeped into her bones. Her heart hammered. Her legs felt like jelly, threatening to give way beneath her. She hugged her belly, trying to make herself smaller, less visible, a part of the darkness. Or maybe she should step out of the alcove and stand beneath that streetlight? Fuck, she wasn't sure what to do for the best.

What if someone saw her? What would they think? What would she say she was doing if they asked her? Her mind raced, a kaleidoscope of imagined scenarios. Prison. Shame. The final destruction of her life. She closed her eyes, wishing she could wake up from this nightmare. But the taste of fear was real, the silent, terrifying wait for them to come back was real.

Every sound jangled her nerves. She scanned the street, searching for any sign of movement.

Then, a new sound. Distinct. Unmistakable.

The rhythmic thud of heavy boots on the pavement.

Amelia froze. Her gaze snapped to the far end of the street, where a figure emerged.

A helmet. A dark uniform. A policeman.

Oh my God…

He walked slowly, his pace suggesting a routine patrol. He hadn't seen her yet, but he headed in her direction. Panic seized her, a clenching fist in her gut. She couldn't make a sound. She couldn't cough. Lenny and Shank were inside, the best place for them, and if she alerted them and they came out, the copper would see them. They were safe but she was exposed, a sitting duck.

He was closer now, close enough for her to distinguish the details of his uniform, the gleam of his buttons. His eyes, though shadowed by the brim of his helmet, seemed to sweep over her, pause, and then return. He changed his trajectory, moving directly towards her.

"Evening, miss." He peered at her in the darkness of the alcove while he stood in the light of the lamp. "What are you doing out here on your own?"

Amelia's mind raced, desperate for a plausible lie. Her tongue felt thick, her mouth dry. "Just…just waiting."

He took another step closer, his gaze sweeping over her dress, her coat, her face. "Waiting for what? Your husband*?" There was an implied sneer in his tone.*

Did he think she was a prostitute?

"Yes." She latched on to the word, a lifeline. "My husband. He's…he's just gone to get something from

his mother's round the corner. We don't get along, me and his mum. He'll be back any minute."

His lips twitched in a cynical half-smile. "A late hour to be visiting his mum. You wouldn't happen to be waiting for anything else, would you?" His eyes narrowed, and the implication hung in the air again, heavy and offensive.

Soliciting.

A flush of heat rose to her cheeks, shame overriding her fear for a fleeting moment. "No! Of course not!" The injustice of his accusation, on top of everything else, stung deeply.

"No need to be affronted. I'm just doing my job. I see a lot of young women like you, all alone in the dark, waiting for a 'husband'. Seems they're always in a hurry, too, just like you'll be once I call for backup. You might even run."

Her stomach rolled over. What did he mean, backup? Was it so someone else could walk his beat after he'd arrested her? Or was it so an officer would turn up in a car so they could take her to the station? Did she even look like a prostitute? She supposed she might, seeing as she had a short dress on, had put makeup on, and she'd done her hair nice.

He towered over her, his presence intimidating. "You wouldn't want to cause a fuss, would you? A *good girl like you. Best tell me the truth, and we can sort this out quietly. Between me and you."*

She had a feeling he meant something else entirely. That if she had sex with him he'd let her go. The alcove was the perfect place, shielded from view. How disgusting was he?

"I'm not who you think I am," she said.

Her mind was a whirl of panic. The jeweller's shop. Lenny. Shank. The police. The soliciting accusation. The sexual proposition. Her life was collapsing around her, and she had to think, had to act. She forced herself to meet his gaze.

"I really am waiting for my husband," she insisted.

The copper's gaze swept the street one last time. He seemed to reconsider, perhaps deciding that an official report on a presumed prostitute was too much fuss for a quiet night, and that perhaps having sex with her wasn't a good idea after all. "All right, just make sure you get home soon. It's not safe out here for a woman alone." He turned, his boots resuming their rhythmic thud, walking away.

Amelia sagged against the wall, a choked sob escaping her lips. He was gone. She'd done it, got rid of him.

But her reprieve was short-lived. Just as the policeman's form disappeared around the corner, two figures burst from the alleyway beside the jeweller's. Lenny and Shank, their chests heaving. Shank clutched a small canvas bag, its shape suggesting the contents were heavy and valuable.

"Scarper!" Lenny hissed, his voice raw with urgency, his eyes wide and wild. "Now, Amelia! Run!"

The command was all she needed. Her legs, which had felt so weak moments before, surged with energy. She didn't look back. She didn't question. The streets blurred into a tunnel of dark brick and flickering lights. She didn't know where she was going, only that she had to keep moving—in the opposite direction to that policeman.

Chapter Fourteen

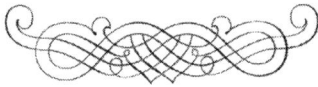

Still in the Noodle, Shank clock-watched. He had to pick Amelia up in a bit. His bitter tasted metallic. His hands trembled a little as he raised the glass to his lips. Old age did his fucking head in. Because it wasn't his run-in with the twins that had him shaky.

It *wasn't*.

Twenty minutes ago, the pub had been his sanctuary, a place to sit and think about what he'd not long done. He'd killed Riley for thinking he could disrespect Amelia, and he'd battered Preston to death and, as always after something like this, the whispers of guilt kicked in: *They've got a mother who'll have their heart broken because of you. You dragged Amelia into this for no reason. You could have nicked that briefcase on your own, she didn't have to be there.*

No, she didn't, but he'd wanted her to see that if he was doing something for her, she could do something for him.

Childish bastard.

After all these years, he still didn't understand himself.

Amelia had no idea of who he really was. She thought he was a robber like Lenny, a man who liked a scam or two as long as it lined his pockets, but he'd wandered down a different path to Lenny at some point, becoming known, on the quiet, as someone who could make people disappear if you paid him. He'd always seen the victim as a mark, a job. The actual killing was fine, he was emotionless throughout, which didn't make sense when he was crippled with guilt afterwards.

Not only was he childish but he was complex.

People chatted around him, but he wasn't listening. The low hum of conversation was the familiar part of his daily routine, except he was used to hearing it in the café, not a boozer. He hadn't been thinking clearly when he'd driven by and decided to have a drink here. How could he have forgotten the twins owned it? Or was it a subconscious thing—he'd heard they'd turned up at the café (Jesus Christ, after all these years of it being a secret), and so he'd wanted to piss on their patch like they'd done to his?

Amelia owed them a lot of money. The amount she charged each person every day, she could probably afford to hand it over to them, clear the debt from when they'd taken over the Estate, because if previous leaders had known what she was up to, then that wasn't her problem. They were dead and couldn't come calling for their money, and the twins didn't have the right to expect it either.

Then they'd arrived here. They were young and reminded him of how he used to be years ago, carrying a heavy air of menace; it fucking clung to them. Sharp suits. Their eyes, unsettlingly canny, had scanned the room then found Shank.

When they'd approached his table, he'd known he'd made a colossal mistake in being here. There was Amelia, usually moaning about the lads of today not being like those in their past, but the twins? They were a curious mix of old and new, probably because they'd grown up watching Ron Cardigan rule the place. He admired them, their brass balls, and was glad they hadn't been around when Shank had been at the height of his profession.

They'd have killed him, no question.

And then the name had been dropped. Lenny Bagby. And it was so obvious why they were asking. They'd do what every decent leader should now and poke into Amelia's life to determine whether she owed them a shit-ton of money. But poking into her life meant they'd catch a glimpse of his—or had they already done that? Had they sent people to spy on him, and they'd witnessed him shooting Riley? Were they going to bide their time before they took him to some hideaway or other and killed him?

"Fuck you, Lenny," he muttered. "Still causing havoc when you're dead."

He'd been gone for thirty-two years. His best friend back in the day, the man whose wife Shank had coveted. Things could have been so different there if he'd grown a set, but he hadn't, and by the time he had, he'd left it too late.

And those twins. As quickly as they'd arrived, they'd fucked off again.

Shank thought about how weird his day had been so far compared to the usual. Normally, he'd be in the café, directing the young lads on where to go and what to do, jobs he'd once done himself. Then Amelia had announced they'd be going to the manor. And Riley had got cocky. The theft of the briefcase. Battering Preston. The shooting. Lenny's name cropping up after all these years. And the twins, asking questions.

It was all a bit much. A bit…busy, and there was still the manor to go.

Was that wise now the twins had popped into their lives?

Something dark was stirring because of the café discovery. And if it was stirring, the ripples would reach Amelia. He had to tell her about his chat with George and Greg. As much as he wanted to retreat into the safe routine of his twilight years and tell her to stick the manor job up her arse, he couldn't do it to her. Not Amelia. Not after everything. After he'd just got her involved in that little sojourn to the warehouse.

He pushed himself up, his knees cracking in protest.

He clocked the woman behind the bar clocking him.

Outside, the canvas of greys and muted browns had him wanting to go somewhere pretty and colourful. Abroad. On a beach somewhere. He drove away, eyeing the familiar streets, a patchwork of old Victorian terraces rubbing shoulders with new-builds. Every alleyway held a memory, and a ghost stood on every corner. This had been his stomping ground back in the day, and it had all gone in the blink of an eye.

The café drew him, its windows steamed, as usual. He'd told Amelia she'd be better off putting on that sticky stuff that turned them frosted. It'd save everyone sitting in the warm, damp air. It wasn't doing Shank's chest much good, keep breathing it in. He knocked, and she let him in, going to stand behind the counter. She was ready for her own shot at remembered youth, standing there in her coat and scarf.

"You look tense," she said.

"That's because I am."

She cocked her head. "Why?"

"When I left after dropping you off earlier, I nipped into the Noodle."

She glared at him. "The twins' pub."

"Hmm."

"Why? Are you *courting* trouble?"

He shrugged. "I don't know why. I wasn't thinking. I never do after I've killed someone." There, he'd let his secret out.

"So is that a regular occurrence, killing someone?" she asked.

"It used to be."

"Fucking hell… Is that why Lenny had a gun? Was he out there killing people, too?"

"It's a story for another day."

"Or maybe one I don't want to hear at all."

"You're probably right there. Anyway, the twins, they came in."

She sighed. "Of course they fucking did."

"They asked me about Lenny."

The colour drained from her face. "Lenny? That means they're looking into me."

"They were serious, it wasn't just some casual enquiry. Seems to me they're after you, after digging shit up. They'll be trying to prove you owe protection money. Are you sure we should go to the manor tonight?"

"Yes, I got Charlie to sort a distraction." Her gaze darted around the empty café, as if she expected the twins to materialise. "This is insane. Oh God, what if they come back? I don't want shit in my life."

"If you don't want shit, then close the café."

"That's my intention—after we've got the suitcase. But back to the twins. What if they don't go away?"

"I won't let them hurt you," Shank said.

He sensed her reaction to his words were different to what they would have been five minutes ago. 'I won't let them hurt you' translated to 'I'll kill them before they hurt you'. She nodded, giving him permission to do whatever he felt was best, but even he knew that killing the twins would have awful repercussions, and now that he'd had such a full-on day, he realised *he* didn't want shit in his life either.

Rain drummed against the windows. Shank went over to one and cuffed a porthole. He looked out into the street. Nothing out there but the lurking shadows. He had a terrible, sinking feeling that they either shouldn't meet with Floyd later or something bad was on the horizon. The twins were going to demand a price Amelia might not be able to pay, considering how long she'd kept this place from them.

"We're doing it," she said. "I want the money in that suitcase. I want out of here." She gestured to the café. "This place. I'll sell it and fuck off."

Shank nodded, wishing he could go with her, but that ship had sailed. He'd fucked up with her years ago, more's the pity.

Chapter Fifteen

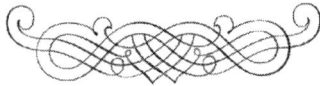

A big breath of wind buffeted George, trying to push him over, and if it were a person, he'd have punched it in the face. Beside him, Greg walked with his head bent into the wind, hands buried in his pockets. The rain had pissed it down on their way here but had thankfully stopped.

The pavements, slick beneath their feet, reflected the glow of nearby streetlamps.

The Eagle's sign swung and creaked. This was George's kind of place, a pub with history, secrets, and regulars who knew how to keep their mouths shut. He hated the fact that he loved it as much as their real father had. This gaff had been Ron's castle.

George pushed the door open. The warmth hit first, then the sudden hush. Conversations faltered. Heads turned. The familiar feeling of eyes on them always made him think someone had done something wrong, but the chatter quickly resumed, putting his mind at rest. He took in every detail on his way to the bar.

Jack, the landlord, stood behind it. He laid a tea towel over his shoulder. "All right?"

"Yeah, you?"

"Not bad."

"We need a word. In private."

Jack nodded. "Right. Back room."

George and Greg followed him through. They sat around the table. Jack looked as if he expected bad news.

"Nothing's wrong," George said. "Well, nothing you need to be wary about anyway."

Jack swallowed. "What's up then?"

George fixed him with an unblinking stare. "We happened to go down a street we never use today. Saw this place, looked like a café to me, but the old dear in there reckons she owns it and it's used as a community hub. First we'd fucking heard of it." He told Jack the location. "I bet you've heard of the woman, and her old man. Lenny and Amelia Bagby."

"Yeah." Jack sighed. "Bad business, that. Lenny went inside for a long stretch. Manslaughter. It was years ago now. And I'm going by gossip, so take this with a pinch of salt: Lenny was known for robbing. One night, he broke into this old lady's house. Eighty-odd, she was. Rumour had it he got spooked because she woke up, or she put up a fight, but whatever it was, he shot her. Left her for dead, all for a few bits of jewellery. The police caught him quick, and he never put up a fight, just let them take him down the nick. He pleaded guilty. Personally, I reckon he had someone with him and took the rap for the pair of them. I heard he died in the early nineties."

George absorbed the information. "Did you ever hear about the hidden café? A place where certain people go, out of the way. A lot of business gets done there, like it used to in here."

Jack frowned and shook his head. "London's full of secrets, but I've never heard of anything like that. A lot of the younger lads keep their dealings quiet, but usually it's a back room like this, or a lock-up. A café, though? Never." He scratched his chin. "Must have been kept a proper secret if we haven't heard of it."

George straightened up. "Well, if you do hear anything, about Lenny or about this café, you know how to find us."

Jack nodded. "I'll keep an ear out."

Back in the bar, the volume had risen slightly. George surveyed the room again, letting his gaze drift over the faces. Two old men hunched over a table near the dartboard, deep in a game of dominoes. They'd been rooted to their stools since before George was born. Perfect.

"Looks like Malcolm's aiming for a high score," Greg muttered.

George nodded. "Let's go and have a chat with our local historians."

They approached the table. The old men paused play. Malcolm, a magnificent white walrus moustache sitting beneath his nose, the lenses in a pair of glasses enlarging his eyes, glanced up. His mate, Archie, drank his lager as if the twins' presence didn't bother him.

"All right, gentlemen," George asked. "Mind if we join you for a moment?"

Malcolm squinted at them. "Are you here for a game or a chat?" His voice was old-school posh with a layer of East End on top.

"A chat." Greg pulled a stool over and sat.

"What about?" Malcolm pushed the dominoes to one side—he must be losing if he'd done that. Sly bastard.

Archie tutted at him.

George dragged a chair over from an adjacent empty table and sat, meeting Malcolm's ancient gaze. "We want a bit of history. Heard a name mentioned earlier, someone called Lenny Bagby. We know he's dead, but what can you tell us about him?"

Malcolm smiled. "Lenny, eh? Now there's a name from the old days. Proper crim, he was. Not one of these flash young'uns with their phones and their what3words. Lenny had grit. Had form, too, didn't he, Archie."

Archie snorted. "Always looking for an angle, that one. Never played straight."

George leaned forward. "We heard he went away. Something about an old dear, a robbery gone wrong, turned to manslaughter." He watched their faces carefully.

Malcolm wheezed. "The papers loved that one. Makes me think of Amelia. I haven't seen her for bloody years."

George perked up.

Malcolm leaned back, taking a sip of beer. "She's sharp as a tack, that one. Managed fine on her own when he went away." He paused, a wry smile playing on his lips. "Even from behind those walls he still ruled her, though. Still pulled the strings. We all knew to keep an eye on her, make sure she didn't get up to anything, if you catch my drift."

"Nope, I didn't catch it."

"Playing away," Malcolm said. "Fucking about behind his back."

"Right. And did she?"

"Not that any of us saw."

Archie snorted again. "I heard she's got a finger in a few pies, even now. Nothing too obvious, mind. Likes to keep things quiet."

"What do you mean?" Greg asked.

"That place she runs. It used to be Lenny's. A café, to anyone passing, but rumour has it the crims go there to talk shop. They have to pay her a fee."

Anger surged in George. She might not be running a café, but she was definitely running a fucking business. The cheeky bitch had tried to fob them off but…

I knew she wasn't on the level.

George contemplated telling Malcolm and Archie off for not passing on that snippet yonks ago, but Greg shook his head. George got the gist. These two were better off as friends, not enemies. They'd get more information out of them if things remained civil.

"She's kept it going in Lenny's honour," Archie said.

The idea of a hidden criminal café made a lot of sense. No wonder they'd never seen the usual criminals out and about—they were all sipping her bastard coffee in comfort.

Something dodgy was definitely going on, and they were going to get to the bottom of it. The hunt for the truth was going to be anything but quiet. They'd make a shit load of noise until it drew someone out of the bushes.

Chapter Sixteen

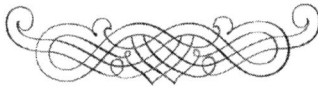

Weeks had rolled by. The day dawned bright blue, the white clouds oblivious to the dark currents stirring beneath their fluffy bellies. Sunlight filtered through the panes of the kitchen window, chasing away the last vestiges of the night.

Amelia continued to carry the quiet burdens of a woman three times her age. She moved down the stairs to the small square hallway at the bottom. A basket of damp laundry, heavy with the scent of soap, nestled against her hip. She pushed open the back door, stepping out into her patch of garden, hemmed in by brick walls, a postage stamp of green amidst the relentless grey of the city.

Lenny had strung a clothesline between two metal poles. She hung the whites first: Lenny's shirts, his vests, her slips. To the sound of the gentle flapping of the fabric in the breeze, she allowed her mind to drift, to conjure dreams of a different life, one where the biggest worry was a persistent stain or a missing sock. But not this morning. This morning, an uncomfortable itch had settled beneath her skin, a premonition she couldn't shake.

The familiar clatter of a milk float in the street beyond the garden wall, the distant rumble of an early bus, the shrill cry of a bird overhead, these were the ordinary sounds of her London, the symphony of routine. Then, a new sound cut through the familiar hum: the unmistakable, high-pitched warble of Mrs Davies' voice carrying over the wall. She delivered the bread for the café each morning and must have heard Amelia taking pegs out of the bucket she kept them in.

"Morning, Amelia, love! You heard the news?"

Amelia's heart gave a little lurch. Mrs Davies, whose life seemed dedicated to the collection and distribution of gossip, was someone Amelia tried not to engage with if she could help it. Thank God there was a wall between them.

"Morning," Amelia called back. "What news is that?"

"A robbery! Mr and Mrs Atherton's place. Poor dears. Not that they need my sympathy, mind you, with all their money. But still, it's the principle, isn't it?"

A lump formed in Amelia's throat. She'd known, deep down, that this day would come, that someone would talk to her about a robbery her own husband had done.

"Oh dear," she managed. "When did this happen?"

"A while ago. No idea why the police are only just passing it on to the papers now. The jewels are worth thousands, they say. Diamonds the size of chicken's eggs, emeralds glittering like the Queen's own. Cleaned them out, they did. Every last trinket." She paused. "And the police, they're saying they have a good idea who it was. Proper villains, this lot. Professionals."

The last word echoed in Amelia's head. Professionals. Her fingers, suddenly clumsy, fumbled with a damp tea towel. Her heart hammered, a cold sweat breaking out on her forehead.

"Do they...do they have names?" She tried to sound nonchalant, but her voice cracked.

"They always do."

Not always. Lenny had been walking around free for ages for the crimes he'd committed.

Mrs Davies prattled on. "The word on the street, from what I've heard over at the butcher's, is that they've got a couple of names already. Been watching them, apparently. Just waiting for them to make a wrong move. It's a shame, isn't it? Young lads, probably, getting caught up in all that nastiness. Ruining their lives for a bit of sparkle."

Lenny had always said he was destined for bigger things, for a life of ease and luxury. And she'd initially been swept up in his dreams, his grand schemes, convinced he was invincible. She remembered the night, only a few weeks ago. She'd been sitting in a stolen Zephyr, engine idling, her hands clenched so tightly on the steering wheel her knuckles ached. Lenny had given her instructions, clear and precise, his voice calm, almost detached, as he'd outlined her role: the lookout, the getaway driver. She had to watch for headlights, any sign of movement, to be ready to pull away at a moment's notice.

He'd disappeared into the shadows, a dark silhouette against the moonless sky, swallowed by the ancient trees surrounding the great house. He'd reappeared, a dark shape again, moving with speed and silence, sliding into the passenger seat.

"Smooth as silk, love," he'd whispered.

And for a fleeting moment, she'd felt a thrill, a terrible, exhilarating rush of shared transgression. But the thrill had faded, replaced by fear. The jewels, cold and glittering, had been wrapped in a velvet cloth, hidden away in a shoebox under their floorboards. They were supposed to be the ticket to a house with a proper garden. Instead, they'd become a lead weight because they were too hot to sell on at the moment.

Mrs Davies' voice pulled her back to the present. "Well, I'd best be getting on, love. Got a lemon drizzle to bake for the church fête. You have a lovely day now."

Amelia dropped a peg, letting it clatter to the concrete path. She didn't bother picking it up. Her hands shook so hard she could barely carry the empty basket.

Indoors, the flat felt too small, too quiet, too full of the unspoken fear that had been festering within her since that robbery. She walked into the hallway. The telephone, a black, bulky monstrosity on a small polished side table, seemed to loom at her. She had to ring him. She had to let him know the gossip.

Her fingers fumbled with the rotary dial, the numbers blurring through a sudden film of tears. She rang the pub. Lenny had said last night he had a meeting there in the back room and he wouldn't be home until about ten this morning.

It rang once, twice, then a gruff voice answered: "Dog and Bone?"

"Is Lenny there?" Amelia asked. "Lenny Bagby?"

"Who is it?"

"His wife, Amelia."

A pause, some indistinct shouting in the background, then, "Hold on a minute, love. Lenny! Phone! It's the missus!"

A cheer went up, followed by the cacophony of the pub, even at this time of the morning: laughter, a tinny tune from the jukebox. There must have been a lock-in that continued even now.

Then, his voice. Low, confident. "Amelia? What's all this then? Everything all right?" There was a hint of annoyance, too, probably at being disturbed.

"Did you hear about the robbery?"

A short, dry chuckle on the other end. "'Course I heard. It's all over the wireless and the papers.

Amateurs, that lot. Made a right mess of it, so it seems."

Amelia's blood ran cold. He hadn't understood. He thought she was talking about another robbery, some bungled job that had happened yesterday.

"No, Lenny, not…not just 'a robbery'. The jewels. They're saying…the police have caught wind, they know who did it. They've got names." She hovered close to hysteria. "They know, Lenny! They know!"

A beat of silence, then his voice, sharper now, losing its easy charm, taking on a hard, dangerous edge. "Amelia, calm down. Who told you this?"

"Mrs Davies. She said the police are onto them. They know they're professionals. What if they come here, Lenny? What if they find the jewels? We'll be arrested! Both of us! I was the lookout, the driver. I was there!"

Amelia could almost see him, leaning against the wall of the pub, a cigarette dangling from his lips, his eyes narrowed in thought. Then, he laughed. A short, dismissive bark that sent shivers down her spine.

"Don't be so daft," he said. "Old Mrs Davies and her gossip. You shouldn't listen to that busybody. She doesn't know her arse from her elbow. And the police? They're nowhere near us. They're probably chasing some teddy boy who nicked a packet of fags."

"But the jewels, they're still here, under the floorboards. What if they search the flat?"

"Listen to me. Nobody knows anything. I covered our arses. There's no witnesses. They can't touch me. And you…you keep your pretty little mouth shut, and everything will be fine."

The line went dead.

Amelia stared at the receiver, her hand trembling. She stood there, frozen, the dial tone buzzing.

His words offered no comfort. He was clever, yes, but the police had a way of catching up with even the cleverest of men. And what then? What would become of her, the woman who'd allowed herself to be drawn into his dangerous life, only to find herself trapped, a pawn in a game she no longer wanted to play?

She looked through to the living room at the wallpaper, the armchair, the trinkets on the mantelpiece. The trappings of her life. They seemed to mock the illusion of normalcy she clung to each day. Outside, the milk float had long gone. The school children's shouts had faded. Mrs Davies had gone off to bake a cake.

The sunlight cast a rectangle of brightness across the carpet. She walked to the window, pushing aside the lace curtain. The street was quiet, unremarkable. A scattering of cars parked along the kerb. But the ordinariness was a lie. A secret hid beneath her floorboards. The police had an idea of who'd stolen the jewels; Mrs Davies' gossip often contained a kernel of truth. And Lenny, for all his swagger and supposed cunning, seemed utterly blind to the sword that hung, thin and precarious, over their heads.

Amelia pressed her forehead against the cool glass, her breath misting the pane. She didn't believe him. Not for a second. The net was closing, she could feel it. And when it snapped shut, it would drag them both down. Her tragic, inevitable fate sealed by a few stolen, glittering stones.

The morning, once bright, now seemed to be the dawn of her undoing.

1973

Eight years of being with Lenny had dulled Amelia's shine. She was twenty-five with not a lot to show for it. Well, to the outsider she had everything a woman could want, apart from the baby, that was, but she knew better. She knew she was being used to commit robberies with her husband when Shank wasn't available, and even sometimes when he was. She was a drudge in the café, just there to hand out tea, coffee, and make sandwiches for people who planned illegal deals to make more money than she'd ever hold in her hand. She collected the fees from the criminals, and by the end of the day there was a tidy sum that she handed over to Lenny.

He'd taken to buying her everything he thought she needed, probably so she didn't have any cash of her own. What she didn't tell him was that sometimes the criminals gave her a tip, as if they knew damn well he withheld money from her. That wasn't unusual, her mother would say it was Lenny's right to be tight-fisted, but Amelia missed the days where she'd earned her money at Woolworths, handed her keep over to her mother, and kept the rest for herself.

Her supposed 'job' at the café hadn't earned her any money once she'd become his wife. And now she was out, in the dark, doing another kind of job altogether. The night smelled of coal smoke and river mist. Her breath plumed in the air. Beside her, Lenny hunched his shoulders under his coat. Shank, Lenny's shadow and accomplice in countless small-time sins, strode a few paces ahead, his steps light for a man of his bulk.

The dull throb of trepidation pounded in her temples. She'd tried to convince herself she was used to it, this furtive dance with illegality and secrets, but *each time they went out again, a slice of her spirit was chipped away, leaving her emptier, colder.*

She supposed she ought to be grateful that she was only ever the lookout or the driver. It could be worse.

"Here we are." Lenny jerked his chin towards a detached Victorian house that stood in its own grounds, its silhouette an ominous presence. It stood far apart from its neighbours, partially hidden by overgrown yews and unruly bramble bushes that hadn't seen a blade in years. The tall, wrought-iron gate sagged on rusted hinges, and a feeble glow bled from an upstairs window.

Apparently an old lady's bedroom.

That was the bit that upset Amelia the most, that she was old.

The street was deserted, save for their stolen Ford Anglia. There was a threat of rain, moisture dampening the silk scarf she'd tied over her dark hair. She prepared herself for standing in the shadows and keeping an eye out.

Shank moved towards a side gate. A soft click, a muffled scrape, and the gate swung inwards. Lenny gripped Amelia's arm, a silent command for her to follow him. What? Why wasn't she staying out in the street?

Gravel crunched under their feet in the short driveway. Amelia flinched with each step, thinking one of the neighbours would come to their windows and peer out. See them. Phone the police. They'd know what this was just as much as she did. A robbery. A violation by breaking into someone's private space. And tonight, with the old lady in bed, it felt particularly bloody horrible.

Shank was already at the back door, a pick glinting in his gloved hand. He got to work, and the lock yielded. Lenny nudged her again to go inside. She wanted to ask why, but now wasn't the time. Maybe they knew there were several pieces worth stealing so they needed a third pair of hands.

Thank God she'd put gloves on.

The three of them slipped inside, leaving the cold night behind. The house was large and full of shadows and forgotten things. The smell of potpourri clung to Amelia's nostrils, and she pulled her scarf up over her nose.

The men's torch beams cut through the gloom, painting fleeting stripes on the wallpaper that revealed faded roses and entwined vines, the sudden flash of a photo in a frame, sepia, old. The ground floor resembled a museum. Tall cabinets lined the walls, overflowing with porcelain, bone china, and silver tarnished to a deep grey.

But it was the stuffed animals that truly unnerved Amelia. They were everywhere. On shelves, perched on side tables, and on the broad mantelpiece above an unlit hearth. A fox, its fur patchy and dull, stood on a wide bay windowsill and stared at her with an unblinking eye, the other having long since fallen out, leaving a black, hollow socket. A moth-eaten white owl, wings spread as if caught mid-flight, its head tilted at an unnatural angle, also seemed to eye her, its glass eyes gleaming with a creepy intelligence. A monkey, its face in a permanent grin, sat on a velvet cushion, its fur matted, teeth long. They all seemed to watch, silent bodyguards of the old woman's belongings, their stares following Amelia as she crept past.

Lenny and Shank, seemingly oblivious to the macabre menagerie, perhaps because they'd been here before and had already seen it, swept their torch beams over the room, searching for the glint of something valuable. Amelia worried about being caught. This house, these things, they were pressing in on her, smothering her.

"Upstairs," Lenny whispered. "She's likely got the good stuff up there. Keep it quiet."

They ascended a grand, winding staircase, each step complaining under the threadbare carpet. The silence thickened. Amelia pictured the old woman, frail and vulnerable, just beyond one of the closed doors on the landing, sleeping soundly, unaware of the intruders. The thought turned her stomach. She'd never liked this part, the invasion of someone's sanctuary, especially when they were home.

They paused at the top of the landing. A glow came from a room directly ahead. A soft, rhythmic sound, barely there—the slow, measured snore of the old woman.

Lenny held up a hand, then pointed to the door. Shank nodded. A wave of nausea swamped Amelia. She couldn't do it. Not this. Not with the homeowner there. The thought of Lenny or Shank, hulking figures in the dim light, looming over a sleeping lady, was too much.

"Lenny," she whispered. "I…I need a moment. I'll just check the street, see if anyone's about."

He glanced at her, a flash of irritation in his eyes, but then he gave a curt nod. "Go on then. Be quick. And be quiet."

Amelia turned and rushed down the stairs. The silent judgment of the stuffed animals seemed to bore into her back as she hurried past. She fumbled with the back door, her gloved fingers clumsy. It opened, and she stepped out into the overgrown garden, the cool air washing over her face. She took a deep, shuddering breath.

She moved through the tangle of bushes and thorny shrubs, towards a gap in the hedge that led to a narrow alleyway. Perhaps she could get a glimpse of the street from there, ensure no late-night plod made his rounds.

Amelia leaned against the side wall of the house, the cold seeping into her bones. She closed her eyes, wishing she was tucked in bed, a world away from this reality.

Then, a sound.

It cleaved the night in two, sharp and sudden.

A gunshot.

Amelia's eyes flew open.

Another sound followed. Lenny's voice, raw and desperate, amplified by the open back door, carrying clearly across the garden.

"Amelia, run! Go home! Say you were there all night!"

Something terrible had happened. The old lady. The gun.

Amelia didn't hesitate. Her legs somehow found their strength. She shoved off the wall, scrambling *through the overgrown garden, tearing her gloves on unseen thorns. She burst into the alleyway, her lungs burning, her mind a chaotic storm of images and questions.*

She ran, blindly at first, then with purpose, pushing herself faster than she thought possible. Her shoes slapped against the damp pavement, each impact jarring her bones. Every sound was amplified: her staccato breathing, the rustle of a stray cat robbing a dustbin. She was a thief in the night herself, but this time she wasn't after jewels. She was running from a truth too horrific to contemplate.

Lenny's words hammered in her ears: "Amelia, run! Go home! Say you were there all night!" The lie she always had to tell if the police came knocking. The thought of saying it was like a stone in her stomach, heavy with complicity. She hadn't pulled the trigger, hadn't even been in the room, but his words had bound her to whatever unspeakable act had just occurred. She was an accessory before the fact, and now, after.

Her lungs burned, a sharp, fiery pain that spread through her chest. Her legs ached, protesting the swift exertion. But she kept going, driven by a terror that overshadowed any physical discomfort. The images replayed in her mind: the creepy stuffed animals, their glassy eyes, the old lady's soft snores, the brutal, deafening crack of the gunshot.

She reached their street, familiar under the dim glow of the lights. Their café, so ordinary, so unremarkable, now seemed a sanctuary. She fumbled for her keys, her hands shaking so much she could barely insert the cold metal into the lock.

The door swung inwards. She closed it behind her, leaning on it, gasping for breath. She took the stairs and walked to the living room, avoiding turning on the light. The faint glow from the street filtered through the thin lace curtains, painting the familiar furniture in shades of night. She sank onto the ugly sofa, burying her face in her hands, her whole body trembling.

The old lady. What had happened? The gun. Was it Lenny or Shank who'd used it? Had the lady woken up and seen them and they'd panicked? The questions swirled.

Her past felt like a distant dream. The carefree laughter on her nights out with Brenda, the naive hopes, they were gone, replaced by the grim reality of this night. Her life with Lenny, built on deceit and robberies, had reached a crescendo. How could she ever look at him again, knowing what she knew, knowing what he'd done?

The night extended before her, endless and black. She had to wait. Wait for Lenny—if he came home. Wait for the morning; would it dawn with a knock on the door? The police? And then, she'd have to lie.

The weight of it settled on her shoulders. She sat there, changed, forever haunted by the memory of a single gunshot and all it implied. She was home, safe, just as Lenny had commanded, but she'd never be the same. The silence of the flat buried her alive in a truth she could never speak.

Chapter Seventeen

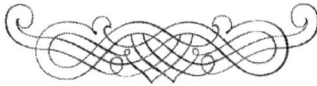

If the weather could make its mind up, about now would be grand. The fine misty rain from earlier had given way to bouts of heavier drizzle, each drop adding to the speckles already on Moody's windscreen.

The old man, Shank, had been easy enough to follow from the Noodle, a slow drive through the streets. Moody had anticipated a return to some anonymous terraced house or a flat, but instead, Shank had parked outside a building on a side street.

Moody gnawed on the inside of his cheek. The twins had asked his cousin, Bea, to poke into who Shank was. That couldn't be his actual name, not in a month of Sundays. They'd come back to Moody with the details. No known family, a basic pension, nothing to write home about.

Moody hated not having the full picture. He preferred clear, verifiable facts. And right now, the fact was, his target was inside that steamed-up box of not-a-café, and Moody was out here, asking himself how long he'd have to sit and wait.

He pulled his phone from his inside jacket pocket.

MOODY: TARGET ENTERED CAFÉ. WINDOWS STEAMED. CAN'T SEE INSIDE.

GG: GO IN.

Moody sighed, a wisp of vapour in the cold, confined space. He slipped the phone back into his pocket, the hard edge of it pressing against his ribs. He checked his reflection in the darkened window. He'd do.

He got out. The street was quiet, save for the distant rumble of the Tube. He took a moment, letting his heart rate even out. He crossed the street, scanning the periphery, muscle memory from years of looking for threats that weren't immediately obvious. He pushed open the café door. The sudden warmth inside was a shock, thick and humid, like walking into a steam bath.

Two old people stared at him.

The place was grubby. More than a bit, if he were honest. The floor looked like it hadn't had a proper scrub in years. The tables and chairs, a mismatched collection of elderly, scarred furniture, bore evidence of spilled drinks.

Moody sat at a nearby table under the watchful eyes of the old people. The woman came over, her gaze fixed on him. The hairs rose on the back of Moody's neck.

"What do you want?" she asked.

Moody smiled at her. "Coffee, please. Black."

She nodded once, curt, then turned and strutted towards the counter, muttering that they were closed and she'd forgotten to lock the fucking door.

Moody pulled out his phone again, filing away the unease. He knew better than to act like he was observing. He opened his Notes app and added some information.

ONLY TWO PEOPLE INSIDE, SHANK AND AN OLD WOMAN, PRESUMABLY AMELIA AS SHE'S GONE TO MAKE ME COFFEE.

His peripheral vision worked overtime. Shank was still there, by the door.

The old dear carried a small cup over. An espresso. A little amount so he'd fuck off quick? She placed it in front of him, the coffee dark and steaming.

"That'll be three seventy-five," she said.

Moody put his phone facedown on the table, pulling out his wallet. He extracted a five-pound note and handed it to her. "Keep the change."

She took the money. She didn't move, her stare a challenge, almost accusatory. Then she turned her back to him and walked to Shank. Leaned towards him to whisper.

Moody strained to hear her.

"...we're supposed to be... suitcase? ...the bloody manor!"

"...wait it out."

Moody picked up his phone and added another note.

They're discussing a suitcase, think it's at the manor? And she accepted cash for coffee, so there's no argument, she's definitely running a business.

He lifted his coffee and took a sip. It was surprisingly good, strong and bitter. He downed the rest while she watched him. The atmosphere had grown heavy, the silence pressing in. Something was definitely off.

He rose and left the café, hoping to never have to go in there again. Back in the car, he copy and pasted his notes into a WhatsApp message and sent it. He also added his thoughts.

Moody: I think they were on their way somewhere when I turned up. Got the feeling I'd walked in as they were about to leave. She had her coat and scarf on, so unless she'd been somewhere while he was in the pub... I'll keep watch. Chat soon.

Chapter Eighteen

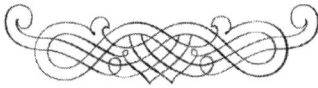

Floyd stood by the window in the study, watching the branches of the ancient oaks thrash in the wind. He checked his watch for the umpteenth time. Six p.m. Were they going to be punctual? Punctuality suggested seriousness, and seriousness meant money. He smoothed the creases from his jacket. What would Amelia think of the place? Simon had moved all of his belongings out and into storage, and Floyd hadn't bothered to furnish it properly himself; there was no point. It was a holding pen, a waiting room until he'd decided what to do with his life. And here he was, contemplating an illegal sale.

A pair of headlights cut through the dark on the road beyond the vast front garden. A vehicle turned onto the gravel driveway and pulled up to the house. Two figures emerged, heads bent against the rain, Shank assisting Amelia by threading his arm through her crooked one. They walked up the steps.

The doorbell chimed. Floyd took a deep breath, pushing down the tremors of anxiety and a glint of hope. This was it. The escape route. His way out of the life he'd chosen but no longer wanted.

He left the study and walked to the front door, opening it. Amelia and Shank stood on the top step. Amelia offered a brittle smile. Shank's gaze swept over Floyd and then past him, assessing the foyer.

"Come in," Floyd said, stepping aside.

They entered, bringing with them the scent of damp coats.

"Nice place." Shank looked up at the empty space where a huge chandelier had once been.

Floyd wasn't about to explain where it had gone. He'd heard the crash as it had hit the floor during the gunfight.

"Follow me, please," Floyd said. "We can discuss everything in the study."

He led them there, their footsteps echoing.

A Home Bargains rug covered the parquet floor. Two mismatched armchairs, relics from a charity shop, faced each other across a coffee table he'd filched out of Mum and Dad's loft. A floor lamp did little to chase away the dark, the bulb low wattage. He blushed at how shit this must look, how cheap, but he wasn't about to spend a fortune on furniture when what he had did him well enough.

"Sit down if you want." Floyd gestured to the armchairs.

They sat.

"So," Amelia began, "Grove Manor."

A flush crept up Floyd's neck. Her stare bothered him. "Yeah, I thought I could deal with living here, but it's too much for me. The upkeep, the size. It's a beautiful house, but it needs someone who'll appreciate it. I've realised I'm better off in my flat."

"These old piles need constant attention," Shank said. "You're after a quick sale, I gather?"

"As quick as possible, yes," Floyd admitted. "How much are you offering?"

Amelia mentioned an eye-watering sum.

"Fuck me," Floyd blurted. "I mean, err, yes, that's fine by me."

She reached into her pocket and pulled out a small phone. She brought up an image and turned it towards Floyd. The screen glowed with an impossible, almost obscene picture. Stacks of cash. Neat bundles of notes, a fortune so vast it shit the life out of him. More money than he'd ever seen in his life.

"As you can see," she said, "I'm serious. In cash, as promised."

Floyd got flustered. "Yeah, well, I mean, I never doubted you had the dosh, but... Where did you get that much?"

"It's all perfectly legitimate, saved over the years," she said.

The words were meant to reassure, but they only heightened Floyd's sense of anxiety. Stacks of cash like that, it screamed illegal.

He cleared his throat. "Well, then. I'm happy to give you the keys once the money has been handed over."

"What about the paperwork? The kind just between us?"

"I'll, um, I'll get something printed saying I sold it to you."

She nodded. He was about to offer to show them around when a heavy, insistent pounding echoed through the house.

All three of them froze.

Floyd's breath caught in his throat. His internal alarm bells screamed at full volume. Amelia's smile vanished, replaced by a mask of anger—or perhaps fear. Shank stiffened, his hand moving to the inside breast pocket of his coat. Did he have a gun? Had the old couple planned to do him over? Had he been so blinded by money that he'd walked straight into a trap? The image of the cash, once a promise of freedom, now felt like a curse.

The banging came again, louder this time, more impatient.

Floyd looked at Amelia, then at Shank, their faces unreadable. They offered no instruction. It seemed like they genuinely had no idea who was at the door.

"I'd better get that," Floyd said.

He walked towards the front door. Reached for the handle, his fingers trembling. He turned it slowly and pulled the door open, just a crack at first, peering into the rain-swept darkness.

Two figures stood on the step.

One lifted a finger to his lips. "Shh."

Floyd's throat went dry. His mind raced, a frantic scramble of disjointed thoughts: *What do they want? Are they with Amelia and Shank? Against them? What have I stumbled into?*

George pushed the door fully open, his gaze fixed over Floyd's shoulder. Floyd moved back, his legs nearly going out from under him. The twins stepped into the foyer, their presence dwarfing him. He closed the door, expecting Amelia and Shank to appear any second. Fucking hell, how was he going to explain that?

"Where is it?" George whispered.

Floyd blinked, lost. "Where's what?"

"Don't play stupid. The suitcase. We heard the old fuckers are here for it. Has it got Simon's cash in it?" George glanced towards the study doorway, where Amelia and Shank now stood.

The pair of them appeared shocked, as if George and Greg couldn't possibly be there. But were they complicit, their fear a clever act? Floyd's head spun. The stacks of cash, the quick sale. Was it all a façade? Whatever game was being played, he wanted no part of it.

"Ah, hello, Amelia," George said. "Nice to see you again."

She smiled, but it was clear she didn't want to. "We were just going."

"Were you?"

"Yes, our business is concluded here." She looked at Floyd. "Come and see me tomorrow."

He nodded, feeling sick. "Um, yeah. All right."

"What, at your *community hub*?" George asked. He stared at Floyd. "Did you know about that place? Looks like a café?"

Floyd didn't know what to do. Lie to the twins or drop Amelia in it? "A café? Fuck no, it's just a meeting room." After all, that's what she'd told everyone to say it was, so as far as he was concerned, he wasn't lying.

"A meeting room for criminals," George said. "To make deals."

"I don't know about the others," Floyd said, "but I just go there to chat to my old cellmate. Catch up, you know."

"Are you sure?" George asked.

Floyd nodded, probably a bit too hard. "Yep. Anyway, I'd best see Amelia and Shank out."

"You didn't say why they're here," George pressed.

Amelia stepped out of the doorway. "That's because I asked him not to tell anyone."

George stared at her. "Oh right...but you're going to have to tell us or I'll turn nasty."

She sighed. "If you must know, we're here to arrange borrowing this place for a party. It's my birthday soon, and I wanted something special. Always fancied this kind of gaff where I can come down a staircase like that one in a pretty dress and everyone stares up at me."

George eyed her funny. "Hmm. And Floyd needs to meet you tomorrow because...?"

"He needs to pick up some money for tarting the place up. Flowers, streamers, balloons, that kind of thing."

"And you can't send it to him in a bank transfer?"

"I prefer to work with cash."

Floyd's heartbeat played up, losing beats every few seconds.

George smiled at her. "Right." He stared at Shank, then jerked his head at Greg and they left.

Floyd let out a long breath, shaking as he shut the door.

"What the fuck?" Amelia hissed. "Did you know they were coming?"

"No!" But he was worried now. The mention of Simon's money...Amelia and Shank coming here for it. These old bastards were stringing him along about the sale. That picture of cash must be from online or something.

They didn't have any money—they just wanted his.

Chapter Nineteen

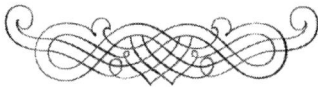

The light hanging over the Dog and Bone's sign splashed a creamy streak on the damp bricks of the building. A faint drizzle sent Amelia scurrying inside to the back room. The usual fag smoke filled the air. God, she'd been so innocent when she'd first come here and sipped gin with Lenny.

She sat across from him, her hand on her knee under the wooden table. He laughed at something Shank said, but it sounded forced, a bit too loud.

"Old Mrs Goodson, God rest her soul." Lenny took a long drag from his cigarette while pouring her a gin and tonic. "Eighty-two, she was. Lived in that house since before the war. Never harmed a soul."

"And to think she got shot for a few quid and a pearl necklace." Shank shook his head. "The world's gone mad."

Why were they talking like this, as if they hadn't been the ones who'd seen the old dear die? Was this what they did in order to convince themselves they were innocent? If they said it enough, it must be true?

Amelia traced the rim of her untouched gin glass. The news of Mrs Goodson's death had hit the East End like a cold wave this morning. A home robbery gone wrong. Brutal, senseless. Lenny had stayed away from the café all day, hadn't even phoned her until this evening when he'd asked her to come to the pub. How dare he leave her in the dark like that, worrying that the pair of them had been caught by the police. Where had they spent the night? Had they got away in the stolen car before a neighbour had seen them?

A horrible thought occurred. Maybe it would do them good to get lifted by the police. It would definitely take them down a peg or two.

Lenny caught her gaze. "Terrible thing, isn't it, love. Absolutely terrible." He squeezed her hand and smiled.

Amelia tried to smile back, but her lips were too stiff.

The door creaked open, letting in a blast of chatter from the bar. Mick, a young lad who ran errands for Lenny and Shank, stood framed in the doorway, his eyes wide and darting. He was barely out of his teens, usually full of bluster, but tonight he seemed scared.

"Lenny," he gasped. "Lenny, you've got to hear this. Word's going round."

Lenny's smile died. Amelia's heart gave a painful lurch.

Mick stumbled farther into the room, pushing the door shut behind him. "They're saying...the police know who killed Mrs Goodson." He swallowed. "They reckon it was you, Lenny. They're coming for you. In the morning."

Amelia's world tilted.

It was you, Lenny.

The accusation echoed in her mind, undeniable. She wanted to scream. Her blood ran cold then hot, a wave of nausea washing over her. Lenny, to his credit, remained calm, his face a mask of hard-set lines. He nodded, a grim acceptance that twisted Amelia's gut. He didn't deny it. He didn't even flinch.

He didn't fucking care.

"Are you sure, Mick?" Shank said.

Mick nodded, still frantic. "Heard it from the blokes on the docks. They heard it from a copper, in confidence, like. Proper tip-off. They'll be onto you, Lenny, first light. That's what they said."

A tip-off?

Amelia's eyes locked on Lenny. He met her gaze, and for a moment, she saw something like sorrow, then it was replaced by a steely resolve. He squeezed her hand, his grip too firm.

Fear pierced through Amelia. She worried for the life they'd built, or rather, the illusion of it. Or let's be even more truthful, it was the life he'd built. Their flat, the dreams they'd once whispered in the dark: a proper house with a garden, maybe a trip to Benidorm in the summer. All of it, in one devastating sentence, was crumbling to dust. She saw it all, clear as day: the police station, the hushed courtroom, the years in the nick, the shame, the whispers, the indelible stain on her name.

If Lenny kept his mouth shut and said he'd done the job alone, then she'd be known as the woman married to an old lady killer. Better that, she conceded, than being branded a killer herself when she hadn't even been in the room.

Her throat tightened at the thought that he might drag her and Shank into this, and she had to grit her teeth to keep from making a sound, from blurting it out and asking him if he was going to grass them up. But he'd always told her criminals had a code, so she could only hope he stuck by it.

Her fingers trembled in his. She looked at his face. Would this be the last time she saw him like this, free, sitting across from her in a pub? Because if he stayed true to form he'd send her home soon, and if he didn't, maybe he knew it really was the end and wanted to spend more time with her before he faced the police. Her mind searched for a way out, but there wasn't one. Lenny's gaze, fixed on hers, confirmed it. Yes, he knew it, too.

This time, someone had died, and it wasn't something he could just brush off like he'd tried to before Mick had come in.

"Right then." Lenny stared around at everyone in turn. "Looks like we've got a long night of drinking *ahead on my last night of freedom. Another round on me, eh?"*

No one contradicted him. No one offered a solution.

For Amelia, the rest of the night was a blurred haze of gin. She listened to the strained, artificial chatter between her husband and Shank. They tried to act normal, to talk about the horses, the football, but every word sounded hollow.

Lenny drank steadily, but he didn't get drunk. If anything, he became sharper. He talked to Mick in low tones, asking about the source of the gossip, the specifics. He seemed to be preparing, not for escape, but for what was coming.

Each sip of gin burned her throat but did nothing to numb the icy grip around her heart. She kept picturing Mrs Goodson, dead in her bed, blood spattering her pillow. The poor woman was now reduced to a victim, a statistic. And Lenny, her awful Lenny, was tangled up in it.

Time stretched, an endless, torturous loop. Amelia found herself clutching his hand throughout the night, her fingers tracing the lines of his palm, as if she could imprint him onto herself, keep him from vanishing into the prison system. She ached for the loss of their future, the one she'd thought she'd have, where she could change him and turn him back into the man she'd thought he'd been at the beginning. But it was foolish to cling to the lies she told herself. Wasn't it better to face the truth? That he'd used her to run the café and had somehow, possibly because he'd been a bit tipsy, had sex with her a few times and got her pregnant. He'd never loved her, not in the way he was supposed to.

She remembered their first dance, the smell of his aftershave, their rushed wedding. All of it seemed distant now, belonging to a different life, a different Amelia.

Lenny finally stood. It was almost three in the morning.

"Right," he said. "Thanks for…everything, lads." He looked at Amelia. "Time to go home, love."

She stood, her legs heavy, her head swimming with gin and dread. Shank and Mick offered goodbyes, their faces pale. No one suggested walking with them. This was Lenny and Amelia's walk to complete alone.

The short trip home felt like it lasted forever. London in the predawn was a city of ghosts. The drizzle had stopped, but the air hung damp and cold. Amelia clutched Lenny's arm, her body pressed against his side. He didn't speak. Out of misguided loyalty, she wanted to ask him to run, to disappear, because wasn't that what she was supposed to say as his wife? But the words wouldn't come.

Because maybe that wasn't what she wanted. Maybe she hoped he'd go to prison. He was ready to face whatever came, for whatever reason, and she wasn't about to dissuade him.

They turned onto their street. The café was dark, seeing as they'd closed it for their night off, its windows reflecting the streetlights. Two figures, silhouetted against the dim light, stood beside a police car parked down the street. Even from a distance, the shape of the vehicle, the posture of the men, confirmed the gossip.

"Lenny," she whispered.

He stopped, his arm tightening around her. No surprise lit his eyes. He squeezed her shoulder. "Go on inside, love. I'll sort this out."

But Amelia couldn't move. The two figures walked towards them, their steps slow, the crunch of their shoes on the damp pavement loud.

"Lenny Bagby?" one of them asked, his face stern, his black moustache tidy.

Lenny nodded. "That's right."

"We'd like you to come down to the station with us. Just a few questions."

Amelia let out a choked sound. "What...what's this about?"

The second officer, younger, addressed her. "If you could just step aside. We need to speak with your husband—assuming you're his wife."

Amelia looked at Lenny. He shook his head, probably to tell her to keep her mouth shut. He took her hand, squeezing it one last time. His gaze was full of a terrible love and an even more terrible finality.

"It's all right, you go on in."

He didn't look back as the officers took his arms. They led him towards the car. He got in the back seat, the door closing. The engine hummed to life, an ominous growl in the stillness. Headlights cut through the morning darkness, momentarily blinding her, then the vehicle pulled away, disappearing around the corner.

Amelia stood on the damp pavement, cold, shaking. She'd thought they'd have more time before they came to collect him. And if she were honest, she'd thought she'd have to endure sex with him, sex she didn't want to have.

The street seemed emptier than before. She could still feel the warmth of Lenny's hand in hers, the last touch, the final tether severed. The future she'd secretly hoped for was here, where he wasn't around, *and it sat before her—until he was released from prison.*

Because there was no way, considering the circles he walked in and the people who came to the café, that she'd be able to start again with someone else. There'd be too many eyes on her, watching, and the second she was seen to step out of line, Lenny would send word and someone would hurt her. Probably slice her face so no man would want to look at her again.

She shuddered. What the hell had she signed up for?

The chill that clung to the prison visiting room was more than just a draught from ill-fitting windows; a cold, creeping anxiety had settled into Amelia's bones the moment the heavy gates clanged shut behind her. It was a bleak Tuesday afternoon, the sky piddling a persistent shower, the weather matching her mood: dank and grey.

She sat opposite Lenny, the scarred, Formica tabletop between them a barrier that offered no real protection. If he wanted to reach out and thump her one, then he could. Not that he ever had. That was one piece of advice she'd listened to. Mum had said it was better to do as you were told than have a black eye.

A black eye meant everyone knew you couldn't behave.

He looked surprisingly okay for a man currently serving a stretch for manslaughter and robbery. He'd got away with having the murderer tag. His defence had been that he was a cheeky chancer who'd broken in while an old lady had slept. He'd been poking into her jewellery box when she'd woken up and opened her mouth to scream. She'd fumbled beneath the bed covers, and he'd sworn blind she was going to bring a gun out, so he'd panicked and shot her so she couldn't shoot him.

All she'd been reaching for were her glasses.

"You're looking well," he said. "Keeping yourself busy."

Amelia managed a weak smile, although the last thing she wanted to do was smile at him. "I'm doing my best."

The truth was, she was barely holding on. Running the café had become a lot without his controlling eye, though she had to admit, there was a freedom in his absence.

Lenny leaned forward, his elbows resting on the table. "Good. Because that's what you'll be doing for the foreseeable. I expect everything to be exactly as I left it when I walk out of here. I'll get my sentence slashed for good behaviour, you wait and see."

She'd hoped, foolishly perhaps, that he might allow her some reprieve when it came to the café, some tiny corner of her life that wasn't dictated by him. But no, the words were out, clear and uncompromising. He wasn't asking, he was telling.

"The café," she managed. "It's…it's hard."

He cut her off with a dismissive wave of his hand. "Hard? Nothing's hard for a woman like you. You've got a way with the customers. Didn't I tell you that when I first brought up mention of the café?"

Yes, he'd been watching her in Woolies. He'd chosen her just so she'd run his shitty little meeting hole. Bastard.

"That's why I married you." His eyes met hers, a trace of possessiveness in them. "You keep it running, and don't you dare let a single penny go missing. Understand?"

She understood. Her job wasn't just to serve tea, coffee, and make sandwiches. She had to oversee his operation in his absence, to be the watchful guardian of his empire while he was away.

"Yes, Lenny," she said. "I understand."

A smile spread, full of triumph. "Good girl. That's my Amelia. I'll serve my time and be back, and everything will be exactly as it was. Better, even."

Better. She'd often dreamt of better, but her dreams never involved Lenny now. They involved a train ticket, a new name, a small cottage by the sea, far away from the grime and the violence and the fear that clung to her. When he'd been arrested, a tiny spark of hope had ignited inside her. This was it, this was her chance. With him locked away, she could slip through the cracks, disappear into anonymity.

But the thought was always swiftly followed by a dose of reality. Lenny might be behind bars, but his reach extended far beyond the prison walls. He had eyes and ears on every street corner, in every pub, among every petty criminal and legitimate tradesman. He had friends, associates, men who owed him favours, men who feared him. Men who would, without question, find her if she so much as entertained the idea of escape. He'd told her once that there was nowhere in England she could hide from him, and she believed him.

She swallowed the bitter pill. There was no escape. Not now, perhaps not ever. Her only bet was to do exactly as he said. To keep the café running. To be the dutiful wife. The idea of living in constant, hunted fear, of looking over her shoulder every moment, was more terrifying than the thought of enduring her current status. She'd do her best with the hand she'd been dealt.

She'd survive.

He chattered on, like he used to, where she just sat and listened, only now, she didn't like the sound of his voice. Soon, the bell clanged, signalling the end of visiting hours. Lenny rose, his movements fluid and powerful. He reached across the table, his large hand covering hers, the rasping of his skin sending a shiver of revulsion down her spine. Now she knew he'd used her, had never loved her, she couldn't stand his touch.

"Look after yourself, Amelia. And look after what's ours."

Then he was gone, his retreating figure disappearing behind a heavy door. She sat for a moment longer, her hand still tingling from his touch, the words echoing in her head: "Look after what's ours."

She rose, feeling the drain of it all. She walked through the echoing corridors, the sound of her sensible heels clicking on the institutional lino, each step a further confirmation of her entrapment. The guards, stern-faced, watched her with impassive eyes.

She emerged into the damp air. The sky was still a bruised grey, the rain a finer mist. The street outside the prison gates consisted of waiting cars and anxious faces. And then she saw him.

A Ford Cortina was parked down the street, its engine idling, a faint plume of exhaust feathering into the damp air. Behind the wheel sat Shank, a man whose smile rarely reached his eyes. His dark, fashionable suit and crisp white shirt had him looking more like a Mayfair gent than a gangster.

Her heart sank. Of course he was here. Lenny wouldn't leave her to find her own way home, although she'd got the bus here. He'd need her taken back to his precious café quickly so she could get to work.

Shank spotted her and got out, offering a flash of white teeth. He beckoned her with a tilt of his head, and she walked towards the car, composing herself, projecting an air of calm she didn't feel. As she reached the passenger door, he opened it for her.

"Amelia," he said. "Rough day?"

She ignored him and slid into the leather passenger seat, the interior smelling faintly of expensive aftershave. He got in and stared at her, expecting an answer.

"As ever, now that Lenny's not around," she replied, her voice flat.

Shank pulled away from the kerb, merging smoothly into the slow-moving traffic. The wipers swished, clearing the fine spray from the windscreen. They drove in silence for a few minutes, the urban landscape unfurling outside the windows: grime-darkened Victorian terraces, bustling shops, the occasional bus.

Amelia's mind replayed Lenny's words, and she sagged under the weight of the enforced responsibility. She braced herself for Shank's questions: Has Lenny passed on any instructions? Does he want me to take over laundering the café takings? Are there any new customers I should be aware of?

But he surprised her.

"You know," he began, his gaze fixed on the road ahead, his hands relaxed on the steering wheel, "Lenny's a fool in some ways."

Amelia turned to him, startled. She'd never heard him criticise Lenny before. "What do you mean?"

He laughed darkly. "He has a good eye for business, but sometimes he doesn't see what's right in front of him—he doesn't see what's important."

He glanced at her, a quick, intense look that prickled her skin.

"What are you talking about?" she asked.

"You, Amelia. He doesn't see you."

She tried to decipher his meaning. Was this a trick? A test from Lenny, via Shank? A way to gauge her loyalty?

He returned his attention to the road, his expression unreadable. "I've always thought you were a cut above. Ever since I first laid eyes on you, looking like a rose in a field of weeds. I've always fancied you. You've got spirit, even when you're trying to hide it."

Amelia stared at him, her composure threatening to shatter. Her mind was a dizzying whirlwind of confusion. Fear, yes, but something else, too, a strange, unsettling twinkle of...what? Disbelief? Curiosity? A desire to see if he was trying to trap her so he could run back to Lenny and say she was a tart because she'd opened her legs at the slightest provocation?

Shank, Lenny's best friend, had just admitted he fancied her. And not with a lecherous leer either. The implications of his words crashed down on her. She was not only trapped by Lenny, forced to run his operation, but now she was caught in a dangerous, shifting dynamic with one of his most trusted men. Was this a genuine confession, a forbidden desire simmering beneath the surface? Or was it a new, more insidious form of control? A way to bind her even tighter to Lenny's world, to use her to his own advantage?

The rain continued its gentle patter against the windscreen, and the city lights glowed in the encroaching twilight, painting the wet streets in hues of orange and grey. Amelia experienced a sense of foreboding, a certainty that her world, already a cage, had just become infinitely more complicated, and far, far more dangerous. Her tragic fate was only just beginning to unfold. The road ahead was a treacherous one, and she had no choice but to navigate it.

Chapter Twenty

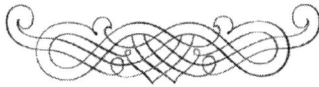

Amelia descended the final stone step of the manor. Shank was already holding open the passenger door of his stolen car. He appeared unsettled, and so he should. The fucking twins turning up had *not* been what she'd expected.

She slipped onto the leather seat, and he shut the door, walking round to the driver's side. He got in and sped towards the open gates at the bottom of the driveway. Amelia dared not speak at the minute. She was angry and confused.

Why had the twins gone there?

Had Floyd got hold of them; was he working for them and had told them they'd be at the manor by six?

No, Floyd had seemed just as startled as Amelia had felt.

Had they been followed from the café to the manor?

That was the most likely answer. George and Greg were snooping around trying to find things out about Lenny, about her, so they probably had someone watching. Shank hadn't mentioned a tail, and she certainly hadn't noticed any headlights along the empty road.

If only they'd heard what had been said as soon as Floyd had opened the front door. There had definitely been some whispering.

For a few minutes, the only sound was the hum of the engine and the swish of the wipers — it was bloody raining again. And another thing annoyed her. They hadn't had the chance for a tour. Would Floyd think it was odd that she was prepared to buy that ancient pile of bricks without seeing all of it?

"What the fucking hell were they doing there?" Shank murmured at last.

Amelia stiffened. The Brothers' unexpected arrival had curdled their performance. She'd tried to roll with it, maintaining her composure, but the twins had been like a pair of predatory birds, circling, especially that George.

"Maybe Floyd also offered the place to them," she said.

"No, something's off. What if Floyd was the one who told them about the café? Or are you prepared to accept that it was a coincidence that they happened to come across it after all the years it's been kept a secret? Bloody years we've been under the radar. And you sniffed out a job, the suitcase, and suddenly the twins turn up, nosing around the same property?"

Amelia closed her eyes for a moment.

"They didn't even pretend to be interested in the house," Shank said. "They were interested in us."

"Maybe it *is* a coincidence," Amelia offered, though the words sounded like a load of bollocks even to her. She knew better. There were no coincidences in their world, only ripples spreading from unseen stones dropped into dark waters.

Shank laughed. "Coincidence?"

He took a turn on the left-hand track, like they'd discussed on the way here. The track snaked between trees and bushes. He kept going but switched the headlights off, the world outside the windows plunging them into darkness. Only the dimming glow of the dashboard remained, casting Shank's profile in an eerie green light. He drove slowly, deeper into the dense woodland. Bare branches scraped the bodywork. Finally, Shank eased the car to a halt, cutting the engine.

Amelia shivered. Through the screen of trees to the left, the manor was dark save for a couple of lights on.

Shank sighed. "So, the plan's still on, then." The question was rhetorical; he probably just felt the need to fill the silence.

Amelia looked out at the impenetrable black. "We must have been followed here. Someone's probably stationed outside the café—that or Floyd told the twins we'd be here. He's a twat, but I don't think he'd double-cross me."

"I didn't see anyone following us down the road back there, and I'd have seen them."

"Not if they switched their headlights off and kept back. Not if they already knew the route here and worked out which direction we were going. They could have taken their time then." She took a deep breath. "There's something I need to tell you that happened, when they came into the café. George looked at me funny and asked if he knew me. Straight away I knew what had happened—he'd recognised my voice from the time I phoned him about Floyd and Simon and what they were getting up to."

"But loads of women sound like you."

That reassured her a bit, but she didn't think George had got where he was today by forgetting a voice once he'd heard it.

"We didn't even get to look round all the escape routes," Shank said. "I've never gone into a property before without knowing where I'm fucking going."

"Do you think they're still around here somewhere?" Amelia asked.

Shank shrugged. "Could be."

"I'm wondering now if someone in the café grassed on me." The heat of anger warmed

Amelia's cheeks. "Anyone could have been listing when I spoke to Floyd about the manor. We kept our voices down, but you know how it is, some of that lot have bat ears."

"I don't know about you," Shank said, "but them turning up felt like a warning, didn't it? Like they were telling us to back off. Or testing us."

Amelia considered this. Did they have knowledge of the money in the suitcase? Had the lad Floyd told about it gone straight to the twins, and George and Greg had bided their time before going to the manor to pick it up? Maybe they only wanted a cut of it.

I thought I'd been so careful.

She turned her head, looking at Shank in the darkness now the dash lights had doused. He was the only person in her life who understood the compromises, the sacrifices she'd had to make. He'd understood why she wanted to do this job, but he'd also understand if she backed out of it.

"So now we wait," Shank said.

"It might be a bloody long one." She glanced at her watch, pressing the side to put the light on.

"Have a bit of a kip," Shank said. "I'll set an alarm for midnight in case I drop off an' all." He reached into the back and brought out two fluffy blankets and some blow-up neck pillows.

"I wouldn't have even thought of doing that," Amelia said.

"The amount of nights me and Lenny sat scoping places out. You learn pretty quickly what you need. There are flasks of coffee in the back and a few sandwiches. I bet you didn't eat anything before we came out. You only ever eat enough to fill a bird."

"Do you ever wonder what life would have been like if he hadn't died?"

"Who, Lenny?"

"Who else?"

"I reckon you'd have left him in the end."

"Really?"

"Yeah. The old ways weren't ingrained in you enough that you'd have been with him by the time we reached the Millennium. You'd have got some fire in your gut and fucked off, sold the place from under him from a place of safety. I'd have likely helped you do it."

"I've never forgiven you, you know, for what you did."

"I know, and for what it's worth, I wouldn't make the same decision now."

"That's easy to say because he's dead. I remember exactly what you said to me after he'd died. The fucking cheek of it."

"If it makes you feel better, I feel a right bastard. I can see how it looked, how it would have made you feel."

She draped the blanket over herself, tucking two corners between her shoulders and the seat. Shank popped the blow-up cushion under her chin, and she closed her eyes. She didn't want to talk about what he'd done to her back then, not anymore. She'd come to terms with it, and no matter how much it had destroyed her, she did understand why he'd chosen the route he had.

It still hurt, though, that she hadn't been enough.

She drifted into the soft blanket of sleep, her last thought of how much she'd wanted to dance on Lenny's grave after he'd been placed in it.

A jarring phone alarm snatched Amelia out of a lovely sleep. She wiped away the condensation on the window and stared outside. One by one, the manor lights winked out. Her heart beat a little faster, adrenaline creeping into her bloodstream.

The house turned completely dark.

"One last check. Are we still doing this?" Shank held her hand under the blanket, his thumb brushing over her knuckles.

Amelia took a deep breath, the nippy air filling her lungs. "We came all this way, didn't we?"

Shank nodded. He let her hand go and reached into the back seat, pulling out a small canvas duffel bag. "We'll have to wait for a bit. It could take Floyd ages to get to sleep." He poured coffee into a flask cup and handed it to her, then he poured his own. He placed his cup on the dashboard so he could screw the stopper into the flask and pop it down by his feet. With his coffee in hand again, he wiped his side of the windscreen.

Amelia did the same with hers.

They drank in silence, Amelia's mind going through the plan.

Half an hour later, Shank put the blankets and pillows in the back. Amelia took off her coat, revealing the dark, practical clothes underneath. Shank passed her a slim-fitting jacket, gloves, a small torch, and a stocking.

Christ, that was a blast from the past.

She pulled the stocking mask on, remembering the last time she'd worn one.

She put on the gloves and jacket, a thrill rushing through her. Who'd have thought a woman of her age was about to break into someone else's property and steal their money. She was older than she ever thought she'd be doing this, but her instincts were still sharp, honed by years of living on the edge.

The cold air rushed in as Shank opened his door.

"Let's go and steal some bloody money," she whispered to herself and followed him into the engulfing darkness of the forest.

The manor waited, a sleeping beast, oblivious to the ghosts of Amelia's past urging her to converge upon it.

Chapter Twenty-One

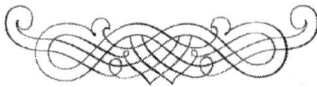

Floyd lay rigid in bed, his pulse a drumbeat. He'd learned to sleep with one ear open, a habit cultivated in prison. Every creak of the ancient timbers drew him from his dreams. Normally, he'd just turn over and settle back down, but tonight was different. Maybe having Amelia and Shank here, then the twins rocking up, had always meant he'd have a restless night, but no. It wasn't the house settling. This was a clinking noise from downstairs, followed by a muffled whisper, swiftly cut short.

Floyd sat bolt upright. His hand instinctively went to the cool, smooth grip of a tyre iron tucked down the side of his bed. Sweat trickled down his spine. His mouth dried out—God, what he wouldn't do for an ice-cold Coke at the minute. He swallowed. He was too tired for all this.

He swung his legs out of bed. The floorboards groaned under his weight, and he froze, listening. Silence again. He moved to the bedroom door, feeling his way in the gloom. He gripped the tyre iron tighter, its weight a cold comfort.

The landing outside his room stretched long. Moonlight filtered through the arched window at the far end. He paused, straining his ears, then headed for the stairs. Each step seemed to creak. He imagined the twins, silent as wraiths, waiting in one of the downstairs rooms, waiting to play a twisted game of cat and mouse with him.

Why, though? As far as he knew, he hadn't done anything to piss them off.

He reached the ground floor, his heart thumping. The air was colder down here. He moved through the foyer, past the moveable bookcases. He checked the rooms, each heavy door opening on silent hinges. Nothing. No menacing figures, no glint of a knife, no ominous whispers.

This was their way, wasn't it? To make him sweat. They were psychological mind-fuckers as much as physical ones—he'd seen that for himself first-hand when they'd gone after Simon.

Maybe he *had* done something and they just hadn't told him yet. Maybe now was the time they planned to do it.

Floyd circled back, his mind racing. Where would they be? The kitchen? Too obvious. The hidden flat in the cellar? The study? He approached it now. The door stood ajar, a sliver of deeper blackness against the greyish darkness. He paused, listening. There it was again. A distinct, soft scraping sound. And then, a whisper.

Thieves? Could this be a break-in? Common London thugs? The twat he'd told about the case? Shit, why had he felt the need to brag?

He pushed the door open farther, stepping into the study.

No one there.

He went back into the foyer. One of the bookcases hadn't quite closed off the room behind it properly. Had someone been in there? As quietly as he could, he shifted the bookcase a smidgen but stopped upon hearing more noise. The sounds were coming from behind the bookcase. Scraping, low murmurs, a male voice, followed by a lighter, more agitated female one.

You pair of fuckers…

He silently moved the bookcase all the way across and peered into the opening. His eyes adjusted, taking in the scene of the room that had once been Simon's fake hospital ward. Iron bedframes exposed their slatted ribs. He'd stacked the mattresses in the corner on the floor, the blankets and sheets on top.

And in the middle of this, two figures, bathed in the glow of their torches. Amelia and Shank, stocking masks skewing their features, were on their hands and knees, peering under one of the bedframes, seemingly oblivious to the fact that he was there.

"Nothing here," Shank whispered.

"He said it was hidden. You wouldn't leave a suitcase full of money out in the open, would you."

Floyd's blood ran cold. The suitcase. The cash. His cash.

Shank drew himself out from beside the bed, dusting off his hands. "Maybe it's in one of those mattresses. In a cut-out or whatever."

Amelia was already sweeping her torch beam under another bedframe. If Floyd left them to it, they'd find it eventually, all that money. But he couldn't let them.

He backed away. He left the bookcase open — fuck them if they noticed it had moved when they made their way out. He nipped into the study and quietly put on his shoes and coat, then made his way out of the manor. Phone in his pocket, he stood in the shadows of the ancient oak trees at the bottom of the driveway and waited for his prey to come out. And when they did, he'd ensure he took back what was his.

Chapter Twenty-Two

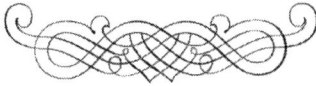

1976

*T*he dawn sunlight bled into the remains of the night-time sky when Amelia stepped out of the café. Mist clung to the cobbled pavement. She did up her coat, the fabric offering scant defence against the nip of the air. Anxiety gnawed at her gut.

Beside her, the faint glow of the café gave the momentary illusion of warmth. She saw it not as Lenny's business and a property he rented, but hers now. She'd make sure she owned it, and the flat above, to stop him from being able to tell her what to do with it. She'd have something that was truly hers.

Shank had convinced her he was on her side, not Lenny's. Time and again he'd shown that, especially in the way he'd warned her about what Lenny's letters would demand of her way before they'd landed on the mat. She'd had forewarning and had been able to get her head around things rather than be floored by her husband's suggestions. But she wasn't playing his game anymore. It was time to take the reins.

Shank emerged from the deeper shadows. His eyes, even in the dim light, held a glint of something keen and dangerous, a predatory spark that both unnerved and reassured her. He held a canvas holdall, its emptiness a silent prelude to the night's job.

"Ready then?" he asked.

Amelia nodded. Ready? She felt anything but. Her stomach churned, a volatile mix of fear and exhilarating hope. This wasn't her world, not really. She was a server of tea and sandwiches, not a nocturnal robber. But the dream of owning the café pushed her on. She'd presented this idea to Shank as her only option. A single, decisive move to free her from Lenny's control.

The plan had been hashed out over weeks, in hushed whispers in the corner of the café after closing. The betting shop she'd picked would be swollen with the week's takings and the last-minute flutters of desperate men. It was a place Amelia knew well now, a place she'd walked past often.

They moved through the night. Amelia's heart hammered in her excitement. Then they stood across the street from the shop. The yellow light spilling from its windows lit up a scene of men bent over forms, eager to win a fortune.

"Stay close," Shank muttered. He pulled a stocking mask from his pocket, the nylon a grotesque second skin, distorting his features into something monstrous.

Amelia fumbled with hers, her fingers trembling, the fine mesh catching on a hangnail. The world blurred through the taut fabric, taking on a hazy, dreamlike quality.

They entered.

The cacophony hit her first: the jovial shouts of men, the frantic scratching of pens, the rhythmic slam of the till, and a dense cloud of smoke that stung her eyes and clawed at her throat. Time seemed to warp, stretching and compressing. Shank moved forward, a blur of dark intent. He was bigger, louder, more imposing than he'd ever seemed in the quiet of the café.

A short, sharp bark of "Everyone down!" cut through the din, sending a ripple of terrified silence through the shop. Amelia walked to the counter, her role to collect the money. Her hands, despite their tremor, worked with speed, scooping handfuls of notes into the holdall, more than she'd ever seen in her life.

A whimper came from a young man behind the counter. Amelia didn't look, she just kept filling the bag. This was it. The line had been crossed; she'd become just as bad as Lenny and Shank by actually participating.

"Let's go!" Shank said, taking the bag off her.

They backed out. The door swung shut behind them, sealing them out of the chaos of the betting shop and into the roaring silence of the street. They broke into a run, the heavy holdall thumping against Shank's leg. They pelted through the maze of back alleys, breaths uneven, the adrenaline a scorching fire in Amelia's veins.

A loose brick in the darkened paving, slick with condensation, shifted beneath her boot. Her foot twisted, pain shooting through her ankle, and she cried out. She hit the ground hard, and another pain lanced up her left arm, radiating from her elbow to her fingertips. Her head cracked against the pavement. The stocking mask, still clinging to her face, distorted everything.

Shank stood at her side. "What the bloody hell? Get up!"

But she couldn't. Her arm lay at an unnatural angle. "My arm…oh God, my arm!"

He knelt, pulled the mask from her face, revealing her tear-streaked features. His gaze dropped to her arm, then to the holdall lying beside him, a dark, bulging shadow in the dark.

"Christ," he muttered. "Right, we can't hang about. We've got to move."

The plan had been fucked up with one careless step.

"The money…" Amelia whispered.

He took his mask off and stuffed it in his pocket, rose, picked up the bag, then helped her to stand. Her ankle was sore, but she could at least limp. Shank flagged a black cab, its driver thankfully more interested in getting home after their fare than in the state of his passengers. Amelia sat in the back seat, cradling her arm, tears streaming, the holdall nestled between them.

The emergency room was a stark, fluorescent-lit purgatory. A few other people sat waiting: a man with *a bandaged head, a child crying, an old woman coughing into a tissue. Amelia tried to melt into the background.*

They sat on a bench, Shank rigid. The holdall lay at his feet, innocent-looking enough to the casual observer, yet to Amelia, it screamed: "I've been used in a robbery!"

Minutes elongated. Every time a nurse called out a name, Amelia sighed that it wasn't hers. She imagined the betting shop staff giving statements to the police by now, describing the masked figures, the holdall. Any moment, the doors here would swing open, and a copper would stride in, looking for them.

"You all right?" Shank whispered.

She shook her head, unable to speak, the pain of her arm constant.

A nurse appeared. "Amelia Babgy?"

Amelia exchanged a quick glance with Shank. He gave a nod. He'd wait. With the holdall.

A young doctor, his face grim, confirmed an arm fracture. The setting of the cast was a fresh wave of agony. White plaster encased it from just below the elbow to her knuckles.

By the time she emerged, she'd convinced herself Shank had fucked off, but he stood by a window, likely watching for the police. Relief, sharp and sudden, washed over her. He hadn't gone. He hadn't taken the money.

They exited the hospital, the night still clinging to the city, the air colder. They got another cab, the silence between them teeming with unspoken words. Back in the flat above the café, the world felt different. Shank, his face carved with exhaustion, helped her out of her coat, his touch gentle. He placed the holdall on the floor and rifled through it, sharing the money out. Then he took his and left.

Alone, Amelia knelt, her good hand fumbling with the bundles of notes on the floor. More money than she'd ever imagined, more than she'd ever deserved. With the proceeds from the sale of the jewels still under the floorboards, it would be enough to buy the café and flat.

She gathered the bundles, stuffing them carefully into an old suitcase she pulled from under her bed. Pushing it back into the dusty darkness, she lay on the mattress, her healthy arm tucked beneath her head, her broken one resting on her chest.

The night had yielded its spoils, but it had brought fear, guilt, a broken arm, and a twisted ankle. She'd bought her freedom from Lenny in a way, but now she was a proper criminal, she'd never truly relax again.

Chapter Twenty-Three

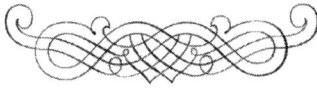

Each breath through her stocking mask burned Amelia's throat, icy tendrils of air snaking through her jacket. Shank gripped the suitcase. It was big enough to have swallowed an adult pig, for fuck's sake, a dead weight, something they'd struggled to carry from the manor.

Was it full of bricks or what?

The front lawn lay before them, the forest at the end.

"Faster, Amelia!" Shank wheezed. "My damn hips feel like they've been replaced with concrete."

Amelia, her own joints protesting, managed a guttural sound.

Every few steps, Shank had to put the suitcase down, chest heaving.

"Almost there," Amelia gasped, heading towards the dark mass of trees that marked the edge of the property. The forest, a dense thicket of ancient oaks, firs, bushes, and thorny undergrowth, promised concealment if Floyd woke and looked out of the window. She prayed he wouldn't do that until they were hidden.

They plunged into the darkness, the lawn giving way to damp earth and twisting roots. Twigs snapped underfoot, each crack sounding like a gunshot in the oppressive silence, reminding her of a gunshot from her past. Poor old Mrs Goodson.

The stolen car emerged out of the darkness. Shank pressed a button, and the boot clunked open, the noise so loud in the quiet. With a final, shared surge of energy, they heaved the suitcase, grunting and straining, until it slid into the boot.

They scrambled into the front seats, Amelia fumbling with the seat belt as Shank jammed the key into the ignition. The engine coughed, sputtered, then roared to life. Shank pulled away, the car rocking and swaying over the uneven ground. They left the forest, and the adrenaline subsided, replaced by a wave of relief. Amelia leaned her head back against the seat, a breathless laugh bubbling up from her chest.

"I haven't heard you laugh like that in years." Shank took off his stocking mask.

Amelia yanked hers off, stuffing it in her jacket pocket. She felt super alive for the first time in decades. The ache in her joints was still there, but it was overshadowed by the vibrant pulse of vitality. She felt young again, like the girl who'd gone to Malcom's party with so much hope in her heart, carefree and thinking life was full of possibilities.

The memory stung her eyes.

God, to be young again. To pick a completely different path to the one she had. She was in the winter of her life, but tonight, it felt like summer.

The car rumbled on, the familiar landmarks of London materialising through the haze of rain. Shank drew up outside the café, and Amelia scanned the street for any observers. Shank watched the street, too.

"I don't think anyone's out there, do you?" he asked.

"No."

They got out, Shank dealing with the case while Amelia unlocked the café door, her fingers shaking. The familiar scent of stale coffee pissed her off—she didn't want to be here anymore. She wanted out. Shank lugged the case in and shut the door. He hefted it over to a table, and she helped him lift it. He fumbled with the clasps, and the locks sprang open.

They both leaned forward and looked inside. Stacks of banknotes. The sheer volume was breathtaking, almost unbelievable.

"Jesus H," Shank breathed.

Amelia ran her gloved fingers over the smooth paper. It felt surreal, like touching a dream. This was her freedom, security, a second chance.

They sat and counted it. One bundle, two, ten, twenty. The piles grew steadily on the table. Each stack represented another year of bills paid, another worry banished.

When the last bundle was counted, Amelia looked at Shank. "Three hundred thousand."

He leaned back. "Not bad for two old codgers."

Amelia laughed. "Not bad at all."

They'd agreed on the split from the beginning. Fifty-fifty. Shank divided the money into two piles. Amelia stared at her half, tears filling her eyes. She could leave this café, this life. She could see the world if she wanted, add the cash to her savings which would fund her retirement. The money she got from selling the café and flat could buy a nice little cottage, perhaps by the sea.

She reached out to gather her share when knocking echoed through the silent café. Her hand froze inches from the money. She looked at Shank, her eyes wide. He stared back at her.

The knocking came again. Louder. More urgent.

Who could that be? In the middle of the night, in a deserted café, with three hundred thousand pounds of stolen money piled high on the table between them?

Fuck.

Amelia's heart thundered. Was it possible a crim had come on the off-chance she'd let them in? Should she open the door or ignore it? She glanced over there. She really should have bought some blinds. Some of the condensation had dripped, streaking clear rivulets down the windows.

And someone stared right in.

Chapter Twenty-Four

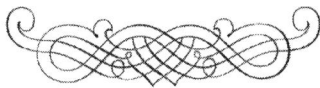

George knocked again, harder this time. "Shank? Amelia? We know you're in there. Time to have a chat."

Still, silence.

"I can bloody see you, woman," George said.

And the money.

She got up and switched the light off, the cheeky bitch. George took his torch out and shone the light in on them. They were gathering the money, Amelia putting one pile into a suitcase and Shank filling a black rubbish bag. Then they legged it to an internal door.

"I bet they're going to hide in the flat," George said.

Greg sighed. "Silly old bastards."

George nodded. "Plan B?"

"Yep."

Plan B meant they weren't invited in. It meant possibly climbing fences, prying open windows, or, in this case, finding a back door. They nipped around the side of the building. The narrow alleyway smelled of dirty bins. George aimed the torch, its beam cutting a white path through the darkness. It illuminated a wooden gate to the right. Greg pushed it open.

They stepped into a cramped yard. Two wheelie bins. Some grass with a rotary washing line in the middle. George took a pick from his pocket and inserted it into a door with a rectangle of glass in the top. The pins within the lock clicked.

George put the pick away and turned the handle. The door opened. He pushed it wider, stepping into a small square hallway, barely wide enough for them to stand abreast. A rack, heavy with coats, stood in the corner, and a staircase ahead disappeared into the darkness above. To the left of the stairs was another door which George assumed led into the café or rooms behind it. Probably an office and a kitchen. If they weren't in the flat then they'd undoubtedly be in there.

George motioned to Greg who withdrew a gun. George produced his own. He didn't plan to kill the old couple, just use it for menace, to get them to do what he wanted.

"Upstairs," George whispered.

They ascended the stairs. George imagined Amelia and Shank huddled together in the flat above, perhaps with the cash between them, planning their next move. Whispering, thinking up a story they could tell the twins as to why they'd stolen money from Floyd.

At the top of the stairs, a short landing with a hallway branching off it. George paused, listening. He pressed an ear to the wood of the nearest door.

Silence.

He tried the handle. Slowly, he pushed the door inwards, bracing himself for what he might find on the other side. It opened onto a darkened living room, the furniture against the walls shrouded in shadows. Moonlight shone through a window, illuminating a coffee table on top of a rug. They slipped inside, moving silently across the carpet. George's eyes quickly adjusted, picking out the shapes of an armchair, a small dining table, a television.

"Kitchen?" Greg mouthed.

They moved back into the hallway/landing. George motioned towards a closed door nearest to them. He headed towards it, Greg covering him. George turned the handle, nudged the door open. Empty. A bedroom. He checked the wardrobe, under the bed. Nothing.

Back in the hallway, Greg kicked another door open with the toe of his boot.

Also empty. The small flat seemed deserted.

"They're not here," Greg whispered.

They waited.

Suddenly, a low rumble broke the silence. A car engine spluttered to life.

George snapped his head up, going in the living room and looking out of the window. Down below, the headlights of Shank's car blinked on, the man himself behind the wheel, his face a pale oval in the dim light of the dashboard. He revved the engine once, then drove away.

George watched him go, a frown creasing his brow. "He's leaving her here? Or is she lying down in the back?"

Greg didn't answer, his focus on the red taillights. The car turned a corner and disappeared.

"Clever old sods," Greg muttered. "Splitting up. Takes the heat off one of them, although they must be thick of they think we won't catch up with him."

Before George could reply, a new sound cut through the silence. A creak. Then another, closer this time. The sound of wood groaning under weight.

George and Greg exchanged a look.

The stairs.

They melted back into the shadows at either end of the sofa that faced the door, guns raised. The creaks grew louder, heavier, punctuated by a strained grunt. Amelia, struggling with the suitcase?

Her silhouette appeared in the hallway just beyond the door. She lugged the case; it looked far too heavy for her, dragging with each step, bumping against her legs. She gasped for breath, staggered in, and placed it on the floor.

She turned her back on them and reached for the light switch beside the door.

The room sparked to life with light. George blinked against the glare. Amelia spun round. Her eyes widened, a momentary show of surprise, quickly replaced by resignation.

George lowered his gun and took a step forward.

"Hello, sunshine."

Chapter Twenty-Five

1982

The bleak light of dawn peeked through the gaps in Amelia's bedroom curtains. It was a familiar light, the colour of her usually drab life and everyday compromises. But this morning, it caught the sharp line of Shank's jaw, the stubble dusting his chin, and for a fleeting, perfect moment, the world felt entirely new.

She watched him sleep, his powerful frame—a man built for the shadows and the rough living of East End gangster life—softened by slumber. His arm lay across her waist.

Certain things had…happened. Obviously.

To others, his eyes held a cold, calculating glint, his smile a slash of danger, much like it had been for Amelia once upon a time. But now, in the quiet sanctum of her unobserved life—the only time she wasn't observed was in the flat—those eyes were filled with a tenderness that could melt the steel armour she'd worn for the years since Lenny had been put away.

She traced the scar above Shank's eyebrow, a white line against the tanned skin. Lenny was still residing at Her Majesty's pleasure, and Shank had filled the vacuum. They'd promised to never tell a soul. It was their secret.

Shank had always been there, a silent, watchful presence, his eyes occasionally meeting hers across the café. She'd thought nothing of it back then, dismissing it as him keeping an eye on her for Lenny, but when Lenny had gone inside, Shank had made sure she was all right. It had started with a quiet coffee, then a discreet dinner, and then, one night, the almost unbearable relief of being touched by someone who didn't demand, didn't instruct, didn't control.

It was the lack of instruction that had been the most intoxicating. Lenny had been a constant conductor, his orders ever-present. Wear this, not that. Say this, not that. Don't talk to him. Put the sugar pot on the left. Why are you looking at me like that? She'd grown so accustomed to the critiques, the undermining, that it had been a while before she'd realised it was slowly strangling her spirit.

Shank, by contrast, listened. He saw her. He never told her what to do, never questioned her choices at the café, never raised an eyebrow if she wore a miniskirt or chose to spend an afternoon lost in a crossword.

He stirred. His eyes opened, and he smiled. "Morning."

He tightened his arm around her, pulling her closer until her back pressed to his chest. His breath warmed her neck.

"Morning." She leaned back into him.

"Did you sleep okay?"

"Yes," she lied. The clock was ticking. Lenny's release was drawing closer, a dark cloud on the horizon of their illicit affair that had lasted for years.

"Good," he said. "You work too hard, always on the go."

"Someone's got to keep the money coming in." And she'd done it. Alone.

Shank's lips brushed her ear. "Lenny always said you were wasted on anything but him." His voice held a hard edge, a hint of his protective nature. "Yet he left the café in your hands. Hypocrite. Have you told him yet that you've bought it?"

"No."

"It's been years."

"I know."

He knew Lenny. He knew what that man had done to her—what he still tried to do from behind the walls of the nick. She'd confessed in the middle of the night once, tears dripping down her temples and into her hairline.

A chill traced down her spine, dispelling the warmth of Shank's hug. Lenny. The man who was her 'owner', as he liked to put it, would soon be here, dishing out orders, ruining the lovely, secret nights she'd spent with Shank for so long.

"I should get up," she said, her voice suddenly businesslike. "The bread will be delivered soon."

He nodded slowly. "Right then. I'll make us some tea. Or coffee, if you fancy."

It was these small gestures that undid her. The simple offer, the quiet acts of service. Lenny would have demanded his tea be brought to him, steaming hot and exactly how he liked it.

She got up, putting on her dressing gown. She felt Shank's attention on her. He understood a woman needed her own rhythm. It was a revelation to be with someone like him after Lenny.

They sat at the kitchen table, sipping their tea. The sounds of London stirred outside. This was their routine, these quiet mornings before he snuck out the back.

A temporary reprieve from the storm heading their way.

Shank reached across the table, taking her hand. "What's the matter?"

"Lenny." The name tasted bitter. "He's…he's due out in a few months."

Shank stroked the back of her hand. "Give or take. Christmas, most likely."

Christmas. The season of joy and new beginnings. For Amelia, it would be the precise moment her hard-won freedom would be snatched away.

"I can't go back to…to how it was."

He squeezed her hand.

She looked up at him, her eyes pleading. "But what else can I do? He's my husband. He'll expect me to be there, waiting, just as he left me."

"And what do you expect? What do you want?"

The truth lay heavy in her heart, a leaden weight. She wished she had the courage to stand up, to speak out, to file for divorce. To sever the ties that bound her to a life that had once crushed her spirit. She had the café, proof of her capabilities. She had savings, a small independence she'd built coin by coin. She could do it on her own, she knew she could, but the enormity of defying societal expectations, of facing Lenny's wrath, felt too big.

"I wish we could last forever," she said. "This. Us. The quiet mornings. The way you look at me."

He sighed. He knew it couldn't last, they both did. He was a man of the shadows, the best friend of another shadow man who'd go absolutely insane if he knew what they'd been doing behind his back. Their little world couldn't continue in the long run. It would be too dangerous to sneak around when Lenny was out.

"I'd better go," Shank said. "Got some business to see to."

The words were a familiar refrain, ones she'd heard often from her husband. In her current world, it was a signal that their time was up, that real life was intruding. Each departure hurt, a rehearsal for the final, inevitable one.

And then he was gone. The click of the door, the receding echo of his footsteps down the stairs, and the silence.

The smell of him lingered.

Amelia remained at the kitchen table, her tea growing cold, and stared out of the window. The grey light had given way to a brighter blue, the sun illuminating the dust motes dancing in the air.

She knew what she had to do—what she should do in an ideal world. The courage was there, a tiny spark inside her, fanned by a dream that somehow they could make a go of it together. But the fear of Lenny remained. His reaction. The task of disentangling her life from his. She loved Shank, a deep, aching love. She hadn't lied to him, she did wish their time could last forever, where his tenderness didn't have to be hidden and her independence wasn't a rebellion but hers to do with as she wanted.

She closed her eyes, picturing the forms, the legal papers, the bold act of defiance. The word hovered in her mind, heavy with implication: divorce.

Her hand trembled as she reached for her cold tea. The morning had broken, and with it, the tragic reality of her choices. To remain imprisoned by fear or to step into the unknown, knowing that even if she found the courage, the love she held so dear was already marked for an end.

⁂

Amelia shivered, doing up her coat buttons. It was barely past nine a.m., but the roads were already stirring, a low hum of distant traffic the only company she'd had for the last hour. She stood, along with two others, outside the soot-blackened walls of the prison, her gaze fixed on the gate that would soon open and spit out a man she'd grown to hate.

Years he'd been inside. Years of weekly visits, of letters written, of maintaining a façade. Years of building something for herself, albeit still inside the shadow of his name. And now, the shadow was poised to fall over her and darken her world again. He'd be there, right beside her, behind her, ruining everything.

A gust of wind whipped a stray strand of hair across her face. Her lipstick, a defiant splash of coral, was an uprising—he'd told her early on, after he'd first been put away, that he didn't want her wearing makeup, and on every visit, she had. He'd likely thought it was for his benefit, her dolling herself up for him, but the last thing she wanted him to do was fancy her. No, she'd worn it as a 'fuck you'.

She remembered the first time she'd seen him. All dangerous charm, leaning against that wall in Malcolm's house. He'd swept her up in a whirlwind of smoky back rooms and the danger of his world. He'd promised her the moon, and she'd believed him. Believed him even when the promises turned to threats, the charm to possessiveness, the passion to a volatile temper. She'd clung to the illusion right up until the day the police had stood outside the café and the dream had shattered.

The gate creaked. Opened. A figure emerged. He moved slowly, as if unsure of the ground beneath his feet.

Lenny.

He was bigger, all those push-ups he did, no doubt. His hair, once slicked back, was now short-short. But the set of his jaw, the glint in his eye as he spotted her, that was the same. The proprietary triumph.

She hated him with a passion.

He walked towards her, his sixties overcoat out of fashion now and too small for him. Amelia had the urge to run, to melt into the city, but her feet wouldn't move. She forced a smile, a performance she'd rehearsed a thousand times in the mirror.

"Lenny." The name tasted alien on her tongue when she was so used to saying Shank.

He reached her, and then his arms were around her, squeezing the breath from her lungs. He smelled of unfamiliar soap and stale institution. She patted his back, a perfunctory gesture, then he pulled back, cupping her face, and his mouth descended.

Oh no. No, no, no.

His lips were cold, chapped, and tasted of cigarettes. And in that moment, as his mouth pressed to hers, a shiver of revulsion snaked down her spine. It wasn't just that she didn't love him anymore, it was worse. She detested him. The touch of his skin on hers churned her stomach. It was as if the last switch had been flipped, and the pretend loyalty, the shared history, the faint embers of what had once been, extinguished in an instant.

She broke the kiss. His grip remained firm, his gaze possessive.

"Amelia," he rasped. "God, I missed you."

The words were meant to be tender, but they scraped against her eardrums. A scream echoed in her mind: "I wish you'd stayed inside forever."

A car horn blared, and she spun round. A black car, polished to a mirror sheen, pulled up beside them.

Shank grinned from behind the wheel and wound the window down.

Fuck, how she loved him.

"Lenny!" He leaned across the passenger seat to open the door. "I thought they'd lost the key you'd been gone so long!"

Lenny released Amelia, a smile spreading. He bent to clap Shank on the shoulder, a genuine warmth in the gesture that had been absent for Amelia.

She slid into the back seat, grateful for the distance it put between her and Lenny. He got in the front next to Shank, his broad shoulders filling the space, his presence already overwhelming.

Shank drove away from the prison, leaving the grim fortress behind.

It was time to climb back in her cage.

The drive through the streets was a blur of brick terraces, steaming cafés, and the occasional bus. Shank chattered about football results, new bands, and other minor trivia, trying to bridge the gap of lost years. Lenny grunted occasionally, absorbing it all, scanning the streets, Amelia's teeth on edge. He was taking stock, assessing the changes, no doubt filing away information for future use.

Amelia remained silent, staring out of the window, watching the city she'd loved during his *absence. The world had moved on, and she with it. During those years, fuelled by a determination to not only survive but thrive, she'd transformed her life. She'd worked tirelessly, the queen of her castle, and now he was out, he'd demote her to scullery maid all over again.*

"So, the café, eh, Amelia?" Lenny's voice cut through her reverie. He'd twisted to look at her, his eyes narrowed. "Shank tells me you've done wonders."

Amelia's spine stiffened. "It's doing well."

"Good, good." Lenny nodded. "Always knew you had a head for business, love. That's my girl."

The casual presumption of ownership, the way he claimed her achievement as his own, grated on her. A wave of anger washed over her.

They arrived outside the café, a world away from the grimness of the prison.

Shank killed the engine. "Right then, mate, welcome home. Fancy a cuppa?"

Lenny didn't answer. He eyed the café's exterior through the window, his expression unreadable. "It looks...different," he murmured, then pushed open the door and stepped out.

Amelia followed, her stomach churning.

Inside, the café smelled of coffee and bacon. The morning rush hadn't started yet, but the display case was already filled with Amelia's sandwiches. A few lags sat around. Lenny walked slowly through the space, his heavy boots echoing. He ran a finger along the counter, frowning.

"This isn't like it used to be," he said. "It's too clean, too nice. I want to keep people out, not encourage them inside."

"It's an actual café as well as a meeting place now," Amelia said—she didn't mention that so far, she'd managed not to pay protection money.

She'd changed his policy years ago, with Shank's encouragement, although the pair of them had kept that news from him. Oddly, no one else who'd visited him had told him about the change either. Maybe they'd assumed he'd given her the green light to make the changes. Or maybe, because of his absence, it was out of sight, out of mind.

Shank sniffed. "Amelia's got a good crowd coming in. There are no normal people, just our kind."

Lenny ignored him. He turned to Amelia, his gaze hardening. "Right, first thing's first. You need to rough the place up again, get the condensation going on the windows. I explained what that's for, but it seems I need to repeat myself: it stops plod from nosing in. I want the untidy look; sling a few crumbs around, leave some tea stains on the tables. Get rid of that poncy sandwich case."

Amelia stared at him, disbelief and fury rising in her throat. He'd been free for an hour, and already he was trying to dismantle her life, to impose his will. But he'd been doing it from behind bars, too, except she hadn't done as he'd asked. She'd gone her own way.

"No," she said, her voice firm.

Lenny blinked. Glared. "What do you mean, 'no'?"

"I mean, no." She stepped forward. "This is my café now, Lenny. I bought it with cash I made from doing a job."

"You own it?" he barked.

"Yes, so therefore, I decide what happens here."

A dark flush crept up Lenny's neck. His eyes turned cold and dangerous. "Your café? You've forgotten who you are, Amelia. What's yours is mine."

"I bought it with my own money." The last two words were spat out, laced with a bitterness she could no longer suppress. "You can't tell me what to do here anymore. I also own the flat."

For a moment, the air crackled with a silent, volatile energy. The crim customers stared. Shank's face paled. Then Lenny moved, a sudden lurch forward, his hand clenching into a fist. He raised it in an unmistakable threat. It hovered in the air between them, a symbol of the power he believed he still held over her.

"Steady, Lenny," Shank warned.

Lenny acted as if his mate hadn't spoken. He stared at Amelia. "Don't you dare talk to me like that, you ungrateful cow. I can tell you exactly what to do. Here, at home, anywhere—because you're my wife, and don't you forget it."

Amelia flinched. All the old unease, the walking on eggshells, the anticipating his moods, of bracing for the storm... It came rushing back, a wave that drowned her newfound courage. The future lay before her as a desolate road. She looked at his face, contorted by anger, and saw not the man she'd loved but a stranger.

And in that moment, as his shadow fell over her, she wished she'd never met Lenny Bagby. She wished she could rewind time, erase that fateful day, and choose a different path.

But there was no going back.

Chapter Twenty-Six

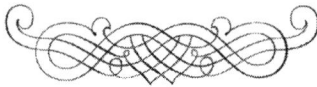

Amelia froze. The words, spoken from the big bastard beside her sofa, sliced through the quiet. She hadn't seen them in the near darkness, nor had she heard them creeping up the stairs. How had they got in? With a pick? She and Shank had rushed from the café and into her office downstairs, waiting until they thought the twins had gone. Then Shank had taken his money and left her.

Her hand instinctively flew to her chest, a gasp catching in her throat.

"What are you two doing in my flat?" she demanded, her voice surprisingly steady despite the tremor in her hands. She tried to project an air of indignant authority, a front she'd perfected over decades. "You've got no business being here."

George smiled. "We've got a lot of business, Amelia. Especially when it involves a certain…theft. What's in the case?"

Amelia's fingers twitched towards it, a futile, protective gesture. "None of your bloody beeswax."

This was *her* money. Her future. She wouldn't let them take it. Not now. Not when she was so close.

George moved then, covering the short distance between them in two long strides. Before she could react, his hand shot out, not touching her, but snatching the case. Its weight, so significant to her, seemed negligible in his grip.

"Give it back!" She lunged forward.

Greg intercepted her, his hand on her shoulder, holding her back with an effortless strength. George set the suitcase on her coffee table and worked the latches. He flipped the lid.

The money. It nestled there in haphazard stacks. Amelia stared, mesmerised and horrified as her dream lay exposed. Her heart sank. This had been her chance. Her one chance to live out her final years with dignity. And now, these two fuckers were taking it from her. The thought sent a cold shiver through her. She was old, yes, but she wasn't dead yet. She'd fought for years, and she wouldn't surrender her freedom without a fight.

George didn't even bother to count it. He nodded. "Right then. Looks like we need to have a little chat about the company you keep. About the clientele who frequent your café. Sorry, *hub*."

It pissed her off the way he kept doing that. Stressing the words 'community' or 'hub'.

George snapped the suitcase shut. "We need to go. Greg will help you."

Before she could process another thought, Greg was on her.

He took her arm. "Come on. Don't make this harder than it needs to be."

"Where are you taking me?" She tried pull away, but it was useless.

George smiled. "For a drive."

Greg propelled her towards the door. She thought of Shank, wishing he was still here. He'd know what to do. He always did. But he *wasn't* here, and she was on her own in this.

The stairwell felt colder, darker than usual. Greg forced her down, her knees jarring with the impact. Then they were outside in the yard. Down the side. Out to the front. A white van was parked opposite her building. It could belong to a delivery service, a plumber, anyone, and that made it all the more terrifying. It was designed to blend in, to disappear, for people not to notice it.

Not to notice an old lady in the back.

Greg opened the door, and she stared at the empty space within. He pushed her inside, not roughly, but with an enough force that sent her sprawling. He reached in and wrenched her hands behind her, tying her wrists with what she assumed was plastic. A cable tie? Then a blindfold covered her eyes. A few moments passed, the twins likely getting into the van, and the engine rumbled, the vibrations buzzing into her backside where she sat on the cold metal floor.

She had nothing to go on but the sway of the vehicle and the terrifying whispers of her imagination. She tried to track their movements, to gauge the direction, but it was impossible. The turns were too frequent, the journey too long.

Minutes segued into what felt like hours. Where were they taking her? What kind of chat did they have in mind? She thought of the seaside cottage again, the crashing waves, the smell of salt and gorse. It seemed a million miles away, a dream stolen before she could even touch it.

The van slowed, then stopped. The engine died. Her hearing sharpened, picking up the crunch of gravel. The door opened noisily, and cold air rushed in.

"Right, time for our chat," George said.

Rough hands took hold of her arms. Whoever it was pulled her out of the van, guiding her, half leading, half dragging her across what she thought was tarmac. The air smelled damp, earthy—the river?

Oh, fucking hell, no. Please, not that…

Then a new sound. A door opening? She was moved forward, then down. Steps. Stone steps, going by the sound of her shoes tapping them. The air grew colder, laden with a musty dampness.

She stopped. The hands released her. She stood, trembling, in the oppressive darkness.

"All right, Amelia." George's voice, close behind her. "Time to see where you are."

The blindfold was snatched away.

Her eyes, accustomed to the absolute dark, struggled to adjust, watering in the light. She blinked rapidly, trying to focus.

A cellar. A halogen light. Stone walls patched with damp, dark-green moss in places near the ceiling. Thick chains with manacles on the ends hung down over a trapdoor. In the corner, a chair. Against a wall, a table set out with tools.

She stared at the twins, their expressions unreadable. This wasn't only a chat. The last vestiges of her hope died. She finally understood. They didn't just want information. They wanted to make an example of what happened when you didn't follow their rules.

And she was it.

Chapter Twenty-Seven

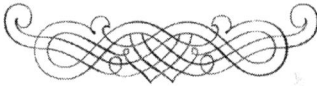

Moody sat in a stolen, beaten-up Ford Focus, the windows fogged by his own stale breath, a thermos of lukewarm coffee clutched in his hand. He'd been watching Shank's place. The street was silent, save for the distant growl of a late-night bus. Would the old man recognise him from earlier, when Moody had gone into the café?

Headlights rounded the corner. A car sidled up to the kerb, a little too fast, too close to the pavement, as if the driver was in a hurry.

Or nervous?

Shank emerged from the driver's side, his movements stiff. He squinted at his front door, as if expecting to see someone standing there, then he hurried to the boot. He struggled with the latch. When the boot popped open, he brought out a black rubbish bag. He placed it on the ground, shut the boot, then hugged the bag to his chest with both arms. He looked around furtively, up and down the street.

Moody hunched lower in his seat.

Shank strode towards his front door, his steps quick. Moody slipped out of the car. He crept silently, following Shank up the short garden path. The old man fumbled with his keys, the metallic jingle loud.

Moody glanced around, checking the vicinity before he made his move. Every single window was black. A stiff breeze stirred the leaves of a towering oak tree near the corner, the resulting hiss and scrape sounding like dry, whispered threats being exchanged just out of earshot. A car alarm chirped, and a scared cat darted out of a bush, disappearing into the shadows beneath a van.

"Shank."

The man froze, his gloved hand still on the door handle. His head snapped around, eyes wide with a fear. The sack slipped slightly in his grasp.

"Who…who's there?" Shank whispered.

Moody stepped forward. Shank dropped the keys, and they clattered on the paved path. He turned fully, facing Moody.

"You!"

"Yes, me. We need to talk." Moody gestured at the bulging bag. "About what you've got there."

Shank pressed it against his chest. "I don't know what you're talking about. This is just my washing." The lie was transparent, pathetic.

"At this time of the morning?" Moody took another step closer. "Don't insult my intelligence. The twins aren't fond of being lied to."

"The…the twins? I don't know any twins."

"Of course you do. They're very interested in your late-night activities. And more specifically, in the contents of that bag."

Shank glanced around for an escape route, but he was trapped between Moody and his front door. Defiance sparked in his aged eyes. This man was used to calling the shots, not being ordered to jump through hoops.

"It's nothing to do with them," Shank spat. "This is mine. I earned it."

"Earned what? Laundry, isn't it?" Moody asked, his hand out, moving his fingers towards the bag. "Let's have a look, shall we?"

Shank twisted so Moody couldn't reach it. "No. Get away from me." He bent to retrieve the dropped keys.

Moody grabbed a handful of Shank's coat, yanking him back. The old man stumbled, fighting, a cornered animal. The bag, caught between them, became the focal point of their struggle. Moody tried to wrestle it away from him. Shank clung on, nails tearing at the plastic. A rip, and the bag gave way.

First, a single bundle. Then another. And another. Cash poured out of the gaping hole in the bag. It tumbled onto the path, a king's ransom on a suburban doorstep. Shank stared, and it was obvious the fight was draining out of him.

Moody stared, too. "Looks like your washing's a bit more lucrative than you let on. You know I can't keep this from my bosses, don't you."

Shank lowered to his knees. "No, don't take me to them. They'll kill me."

"That's entirely up to you. Depends what you have to say." Moody grabbed Shank by the arm, pulling him none too gently to his feet. He gestured at the scattered money. "Pick it up. Every last note."

The journey to the warehouse was a tense, silent affair. Shank, his spirit clearly crushed, sat in the passenger seat, his arms looped around the now partially mended sack. Moody had used some silver tape from the glove compartment after he'd bound Shank's wrists. In the absence of a blindfold, he'd slapped some over Shank's eyes. It'd sting like a fucker when it got ripped off. The old man might find himself with no eyebrows.

Moody drove, his attention fixed on the rain-slicked road, his mind racing. The money. It was more than he'd imagined. Tens of thousands,

EMMY ELLIS

easily. Although he already knew the answer, as he'd received a message from the twins, he still had the perverse need to ask Shank a question.

"Where did you get the money?"

No answer.

Moody tried again. "I imagine you know a lot about this sort of stuff. Theft. Being awake in the middle of the night, up to shit."

"I've seen a few things in my time," Shank admitted. "The world's a big pie, and some people are better at getting a bigger slice than others. Doesn't always happen fair and square."

"So you're saying it's okay to rob someone?" Moody asked.

"It's neither right nor wrong, it just is."

"How many years have you been doing this?"

"Too fucking long."

"What else do you get up to?"

"Nowadays? Fuck all. But back then... You'd have shit your pants if you ever met me in the dark."

Moody could well imagine Shank being someone to fear in his heyday, but not now. But maybe, because Moody had the twins behind him all the way, he tended not to let anyone scare him.

280

The warehouse loomed ahead, a hulk under the low-hanging clouds. Moody drove up to the door and cut the engine.

"Listen to me," he said. "You tell them everything. Don't hold back. Don't lie. Every penny you took, every detail of how you took it. I imagine your life depends on it."

Moody got out and reached in for the bag. George appeared at the warehouse door. He must have been keeping watch on the CCTV monitor in the cellar.

"Moody," George said. "Ah, you brought a guest." His gaze snapped to Shank still in the car, then to the sack. He walked to the passenger side and hauled the old man out. "All right?" he said close to his ear.

"It doesn't have to be like this," Shank said.

"Oh, but it does."

They all went down to the cellar. Moody wasn't usually required to stay, but maybe they needed him. A knot tightened in his stomach. He'd done his job. He'd delivered the old man and the money. Now he just wanted to go home.

George ripped the tape off the old man's eyes, and once the cry of pain subsided, Shank looked around at everything. It didn't seem like he was the type to give the twins what they wanted. Moody reckoned the old boy would rather die. He seemed to know what would happen. The night was going to stretch out, and the only promise would be that of agony and bloodshed.

Moody shuddered.

Chapter Twenty-Eight

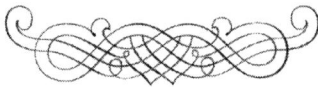

1983

*A*melia's spirit was almost dead these days. She stared out of the flat window, out onto the street. The first day of the year had never seemed so shit.

She turned and sat on the sill. On the sofa, where he'd collapsed last night after a New Year's Eve party, Lenny stirred, a low grunt escaping his lips. Amelia stiffened, held her breath, waiting for the weight of sleep to reclaim him. After a moment, his breathing deepening into a rhythmic snore. Only then did she allow herself to exhale.

It had only been days since Lenny had walked out of prison, a free man. He'd already jumped into a tangled web of jobs and become a detested presence in her flat, in her soul. He'd done his time, he'd said, clean slate. But the slate was never truly clean. The incarceration had carved lines of suspicion into his face, sharpened the edges of his temper, and tightened his grip on everything he considered his.

And Amelia was top of that list.

She slipped out of the room, her bare feet silent on the carpet. In the kitchen, the smell of stale cigarette smoke clung to the air from Lenny's early morning boozing. Amelia moved through the motions of making a brew, her fingers brushing the teapot, the routine a balm to her frayed nerves—only Shank wasn't here to share the pot with her. She filled the kettle. Her reflection in the window showed dark circles beneath her eyes. Restless nights. Her mouth drooped.

She made the tea, cradled her cup, letting the warmth seep into her hands. Her mind drifted past the present moment, past the walls of this flat, past the *presence of the man in the next room, and landed in the memory of another man.*

Shank.

His name was a caress on her tongue, even unspoken. Shank, Lenny's best friend, his right-hand man before the prison stint had sent them different ways. Shank, with his easy laugh, his kind eyes that truly saw her, not just the role she played. It had been a slow burn, their connection, igniting in the long, lonely years Lenny was away. A look, a shared smile, then the rest.

The affair had been a snatching of joy. Stolen nights. Laughter. The way he'd touched her, nothing like Lenny's possessive grip. Shank had seen the Amelia underneath the wife, the woman who craved intelligent conversation and shared dreams.

But it had to stop.

A hushed conversation in the back room of the Dog and Bone when Lenny had nipped to the loo had shattered her whole world. She'd known they couldn't continue, despite wanting to, regardless of whether Lenny was free now.

"He'll kill us both, Amelia," Shank had said, his eyes shadowed with concern for her. "He's different now. And I think he knows. About us. He doesn't know-know, but he feels it. I can see it on his

face when he looks at us together. Christ, you know what he's capable of."

And she did. She knew Lenny's rage when he felt betrayed. Staying with him had become a form of penance, a desperate act of self-preservation.

She'd nodded, tears stinging her eyes.

Since then, their interactions had been a masterclass in polite distance. Shank still came to the flat, for a drink with Lenny, and to the café to discuss the business he'd built for himself once his sidekick had been sent down. Each time she saw him, Amelia's heart flipped. She'd smile, offer Shank a cuppa, their eyes carefully skirting each other, unspoken emotion separating them.

The effort was exhausting.

Now, as her tea cooled in her hands, she winced. Lenny's heavy footsteps in the hallway. The moment of peace was over. The performance was about to begin.

"Morning, love," Lenny boomed. He filled the kitchen doorway, a broad, imposing figure in his rumpled yesterday clothes. His face, though still handsome in a rugged way, bore a hardness around the mouth, an alertness in the eyes that missed nothing.

"Morning." She poured him a cup of tea, wishing it was for Shank instead.

He took the cup and found a packet of cigarettes from a drawer. He lit one, the flare of the match illuminating the corner of his eye, revealing a network of fine lines. Amelia busied herself with frying bacon for his breakfast, a welcome distraction. She talked about the weather, about a dress she'd seen, boring chat designed to fill the silence, to deflect any deeper probing on his part.

Later, after he'd left for 'business', Amelia stood at the window, watching his departure. He drove off in a polished black car, a symbol of his newly regained status. The moment he was out of sight, she crumbled. Her shoulders slumped, her body heavy with the burden of pretending.

She went to their bedroom, pulling back the heavy curtains to let the light in. She picked up a framed photograph from the bedside table, one she'd taken out of the drawer where it had hidden for years. Their wedding day. She looked so young, so hopeful, beaming up at Lenny. So stupid. Trusting.

A sob caught in her throat. She clamped a hand over her mouth, biting down hard to stifle the sound. She wouldn't cry. She wouldn't. Crying was for those who hadn't yet learned the art of silent suffering.

But the tears came anyway, hot and relentless, streaming down her cheeks. She buried her face in her hands, her body shaking with the force of her grief. She cried for the woman she once was, for the dreams she'd dared to nurture, for the future she'd briefly glimpsed with Shank. She cried for the constant fear that one careless word, one accidental glance, would unravel the delicate tapestry of lies she'd woven around herself. And she cried for Shank, for the anguish she knew he must carry, too. The cruel irony of their situation, bound by a love they couldn't express, separated by a man they'd both come to dislike.

When the storm finally subsided, leaving her raw and aching, she stared at her reflection in the dressing table mirror. Who was this blotchy, red-eyed woman?

Throwing off the self-pity, she marched into the kitchen, the scent of Lenny's lingering cigarette smoke a reminder of his presence. Today, she'd start again. Be someone she didn't want to be. She'd leave the running of the café to Shank for a few hours. She'd iron Lenny's shirts, prepare his dinner, and later, listen to his stories of what he'd got up to today. She'd smile. Ask questions, feign interest, be the perfect wife, the picture of contentment.

She'd be the woman who loved her husband.

Amelia picked up a duster, her heart forever broken, a million mute surrenders in her future. And she was both a victim and an accomplice in allowing society—and her husband—to dictate what she did. But that was a lie, wasn't it? This wasn't the sixties anymore, where divorce was a bad taste in the mouth. It was the eighties, and it had become more and more acceptable.

The problem was, it was just as Shank had said: if they didn't stay away from each other, Lenny would kill them.

So why didn't they run? Or get rid of him permanently?

She'd begun to realise Shank might not want her for keeps after all. This was the perfect opportunity for him to cut ties with her under the guise that his best friend would hurt her if she ever tried to fly free. Shank was saying he cared too much for her to allow Lenny to wrap his hands around her throat. But what about the harm he was doing mentally?

It cut deep to know the truth of it—that her former lover would prefer not to rock the boat than make waves for the woman he supposedly loved.

***

Later that evening, Lenny was ensconced in his armchair, a cloud billowing around his head from the filter-tipped coffin nail between his fingers. The *television droned, filling the silence between them, a silence Amelia would no longer break first.*

She stood by the living room window, seemingly watching the rain-slicked street, but her gaze was pointed inwards. She remembered a girl with stars in her eyes and a heart full of possibility. That girl was long gone, buried under layers of Lenny's expectations, his criticisms.

She turned to sit on the sill. He cleared his throat—her skin crawled—and flicked ash into the crystal ashtray on the arm of his chair. He didn't look at her; for all his bluster about her being his wife, tonight she was just a piece of furniture.

As the scent of tobacco filled her nostrils and his grating cough echoed, a thought whispered: He has to die.

It had been brewing for years, a slow-release poison in her mind, but today, it had crystallised. It wasn't a fantasy anymore but a choice: either Lenny ceased to exist, or Amelia would die a slow death inside while her body continued to walk, talk, and force a smile.

She stared outside again. The rain intensified, splashing into gutter puddles. How had it come to this? How had the grand adventure of life dwindled to this single contemplation? She'd tried to make herself love him again, even years back when he'd been inside, but Lenny was a black hole sucking in all light and joy.

The idea of his death wasn't abhorrent. It was practical. A solution.

How would she do it? Poison? Something untraceable, slipped into his morning cuppa, disguised in his evening meal. She pictured the small, dark vial, the careful measuring, the tremor of her hand as she administered the liquid that would take him to Hell and her to freedom.

Or an accident? A slipped step on the stairs, a tragic fall in the garden. She ran through the scenarios. The discovery of his body. Her feigned grief. The police. The questions. The assessing eyes of a detective. They'd pick apart her life, searching for a motive, for cracks in her armour.

She didn't want to live her life looking over her shoulder. The fear of every knock on the door, every flashing light, every siren, the worry that even years later, she'd get caught. Yes, Lenny would be dead, but what kind of freedom would that be?

Her imagination painted two canvases. On one, Lenny was gone. The quiet hum of the fridge would replace his rasping cough. The flat would smell clean, of fresh air, not stale smoke. She'd wake up and breathe for the first time in years. But then the shadows would creep in. The suspicion, the guilt, the constant paranoia. She'd be haunted by her own conscience, by the threat of discovery.

On the other canvas, Lenny remained. His familiar slump in the armchair, the television murmuring, the plume of smoke. She'd continue to cook his meals, iron his shirts, listen to his complaints, and offer the required nods of agreement. She'd force a smile, a thin, brittle thing widening across her stiff face, hiding the screaming emptiness within. Her body would move through the motions, but that once vibrant girl would be dead. This was the anticipated drowning. No fear of the police, just the fear of herself, of the woman she'd become. Hollowed out. Resigned.

Both paths led to a kind of death. One swift and definitive, the other a slow decay.

Lenny coughed again, a particularly wet, phlegmy sound. He stubbed out the cigarette, then reached for the pack, his fingers fumbling. "Another cup of tea," he grunted, not looking at her.

She took a breath, forcing her lungs to process the stale air. Her gaze fixed on the cigarette he was lighting, the small flare of the match. He smoked incessantly. Two packs a day, sometimes more, especially if he was stressed or bored. Or drunk.

A new thought unfurled. It wasn't an active plot, not a crime she'd commit. It was a passive hope, a surrender to a darker, more patient force.

Lung cancer.

A gradual killer, a brutal end, but a natural one. No police, no suspicion, no living life looking over her shoulder. Just the waiting. The quiet, desperate waiting. If he even got cancer. Knowing her luck, he wouldn't. Would there be a long, painful decline? She didn't want to wish suffering on anyone, but death brought on by his own habit offered a perverse kind of comfort. It was a third path, a grim compromise. She wouldn't have to plot anything; she'd just have to hope.

She'd pretend to be devoted to him, bide her time. This was her choice. To live a sad life, stuck with him. Cancer was a morbid, secret hope she'd carry, buried deep. It was an unspoken promise: freedom would come, eventually, she just had to wait for it.

"Amelia? The tea?" Lenny's voice, sharper now, pulled her back into his world.

She turned from the window. A faint smile touched her lips. This was her new normal. This was the compromise.

"Yes, Lenny," she said.

She moved towards the door and glanced back at him. He was already engrossed in the television again, smoke swirling around his head, utterly oblivious to her hatred of him. Yes, she'd wait. For the cough to deepen, for the breathing to become more laboured, for the inevitable diagnosis to arrive. It was a terrible, dark hope, but it was all she had left.

1993

Ten years since the wish had first bloomed in the dark corners of her mind, a venomous, beautiful flower. Now, it was finally bearing fruit. At forty-five, she wasn't so ancient. She could start again with someone new. No one had taken her fancy, and Shank wasn't on her radar, not since she'd realised he'd used her while Lenny had been locked in a cell. He hadn't loved her at all—or not enough anyway.

She sat by the hospital bed, her hands clasped loosely in her lap. The hiss of the ventilator was the only sound, a mechanical breath for a man who could no longer inhale his own. Lenny lay there, skeletal beneath a thin white sheet, his parchment skin stretched taut over prominent bones. The cancer, that much-wished-for guest, had consumed him from the inside out, just as his control had consumed her life.

His eyes were closed, the lids bruised yellow. A tube snaked from his mouth, another from his nose, connecting him to the array of machines that charted his final moments. His chest rose and fell, a movement not his own, and Amelia experienced a sense of triumph. No tears, no grief, not even an inkling of pity.

Why should she cry for a man who'd never mourned their baby?

A soft knock interrupted the rhythm of the ventilator. Shank stepped in. He was a good man, in theory. Kind, often thoughtful, but irrevocably weak when it came to matters of the heart.

"Amelia," he greeted quietly, as if afraid to disturb the dying man.

His eyes met hers. He looked tired, his usually neat hair dishevelled, his suit jacket rumpled. He'd been coming here every day, a loyal friend to the very end. Or so it seemed.

It hadn't been loyal of him to fuck Lenny's wife. To use her.

She offered him a polite smile. "Shank."

He pulled up a plastic chair, positioning it beside hers. They sat in silence. Shank reached out, his hand hovering before gently covering hers, his touch warm.

Shame she still craved it.

"He's holding on," Shank whispered.

"He always was a stubborn bastard."

Ten years she'd spent sitting, waiting, enduring. Lenny's control had seeped into every corner of her life, from her wardrobe to the words she was allowed to utter in public, he'd dictated it all, and she'd let him think he'd broken her spirit. She'd mimicked the emotions he'd expected, nodded at the right times. And all the while, the wish she'd made had quietly simmered, a dark secret, her only true possession.

Shank's gaze lay heavy on her. He always watched her lately. The history between them, that silent, half-formed narrative had never been allowed to fully unfold. She cast her mind back, to the night Lenny had fucked off to Liverpool for a few days. Business, so he'd said. Shank had come over to the flat, presumably under Lenny's orders to make sure she didn't go out and, God forbid, actually have some fun. They'd shared a bottle of wine, and the conversation had drifted from trivialities to confessions.

He'd spoken of his admiration for her resilience. He'd reached for her hand, his thumb tracing patterns on her palm, sending shivers through her.

"I thought we were over," she'd said. "Yet here you are, plying me with wine. What, is this how you

want it? A quick fuck when the cat's away? I'm only good for it if Lenny's not around?"

"I didn't come here for that. Lenny's my best friend. I couldn't...wouldn't do that to him."

She'd laughed. "You already have."

He'd chosen loyalty to Lenny over the possibility of a life with her. He'd seen the truth of her situation, acknowledged it, yet had been too weak to act. He'd left shortly after her outburst, leaving her alone in the quiet. The next day, he'd called round with flowers and an apology couched in vague terms about 'misunderstandings'. She'd accepted it outwardly, but something inside had hardened further. She'd resolved then that if freedom were to come, it would not be handed to her by a man.

Now, years later, that scene felt distant, almost unreal.

Lenny stirred.

Shank squeezed her hand again. "Why won't he just go?"

Lenny was beyond fighting now. He was a body kept alive by machines. She caught the subtle change in his breathing pattern, the small clench in his jaw — had he heard what Shank had said? Heard the annoyance in his voice? She'd studied Lenny for so long, learned to read his moods from the slightest twitch of an eyebrow, the minute shift in his posture. Now, she read the language of his dying.

He'd go knowing they both wanted him to.

"I hate you, Lenny," she said. "Fucking hate you."

His jaw twitched again.

The minutes trundled on. The clock on the wall mocked her with its slow march. A dull ache throbbed in her back, her neck stiff, but she wouldn't move.

Not now. Not when the end was so close.

A doctor, a young woman, poked her head in. "Just checking in. Let us know if anything changes."

"Thank you," Amelia said.

The nurse left.

They waited. Shank shifted restlessly, clearing his throat. Then a long, drawn-out shudder rippled through Lenny. His chest heaved and then went still. The rhythmic hiss of the ventilator continued for a moment, an empty breath, before the sound sharpened into a high-pitched wail.

It was done.

Shank got up to get the nurse. A dizzying sense of release whipped through Amelia. The invisible chains that had bound her had finally broken apart, the links flying. She looked at Lenny's lifeless face, and for the first time in years, she felt truly free.

The nurses came in, no rush, followed by the doctor. They checked, confirmed, and then called the time.

"I'm so sorry, Mrs Bagby. He's gone."

I'm not sorry.

Amelia nodded, her eyes dry. She stood. Shank, who'd risen with her, put an arm around her shoulders, a gesture of comfort that felt strangely possessive now. The same kind as Lenny's.

In the corridor, he whispered, "Now he's gone, can we…can we continue where we left off?"

He looked at her, expectant, as if the past few years had been an intermission and they could pick up the threads of a story he'd once discarded. As if he'd waited for his friend to die, just so he could claim her.

She met his gaze and removed his arm from her shoulders. "No. You didn't want me back then, you were too afraid of him to take me. You made your choice. You chose loyalty to him over everything else. You didn't want me when it mattered, when it would have required courage, so you won't get me now, when it's convenient. I'm not someone you can just pick back up once the coast is clear."

His face fell. He opened his mouth to protest, but she cut him off.

"I've waited years for this day, years of enduring, of biding my time like you told me to. My freedom was hard-won, and it belongs only to me. Not to any man."

She turned from him, walking down the corridor, leaving the hushed voices of the medical staff, the lingering scent of sickness, and the stunned, defeated figure of Shank behind her.

She headed towards the exit, the night, a future she'd sculpt with her own hands. The air outside was cool, crisp. She took a deep breath, filling her lungs, tasting a freedom she'd paid for with years of quiet suffering and a single, dark wish.

The waiting was over. Her life was now her own.

Chapter Twenty-Nine

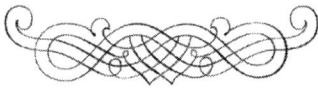

George stood in front of Shank and Amelia who leaned against the wall behind the trapdoor. Greg stood close by, and Moody sat on the chair by the tool table. Greg polished a large, heavy wrench with a cloth. Shank stared straight ahead, his jaw set. Beside him, Amelia watched the twins with an unnervingly calm gaze.

This woman had serious balls.

"So, Shank." George smiled. "Our man found you with a black bag, full to the brim."

Shank remained silent. His eyes, clouded by the years, swivelled towards George, then back to something beyond him. Maybe the monitor at the bottom of the stairs that showed the front of the warehouse.

Perhaps he prayed for someone to walk by and rescue him.

George took a step closer. "You were asked about the bag. Why you had it."

Still nothing. Shank's silence was a wall, built brick by brick over decades of keeping secrets. He refused to engage in a pantomime he'd likely seen a hundred times over.

"Maybe he really doesn't know what you're on about," Greg said, sarcasm high.

"He knows. He knows a lot of things. Don't you, Shank?"

Shank cleared his throat. "The past is the past. I find it's best not to harp on about it, even when that past was only an hour ago."

"The past is the past, is it?" Greg chuckled and twirled the wrench between his fingers.

"Funny, that's what a lot of people have said when our men have been asking about Lenny."

At the mention of the name, Shank's head snapped up. "The past is best left buried."

"We're not here for ancient history," George said, his patience wearing thin. "We're here to chat about the money. Money that was in a suitcase. Money that went missing from a very specific place. And you, Shank, were seen in the vicinity."

Floyd had messaged to say they'd stolen his cash.

Amelia pushed off the wall. "He didn't take the suitcase."

George shifted his gaze to her. "And how would you know that?"

"Because I did."

Greg stopped polishing the wrench. "Why?"

Amelia took a deep breath. "Floyd had it coming. He pissed me off with his attitude. Then he sat there, bragging about it, and I wanted to wipe that smug smile off his face."

Greg stared at her. "From what we've gathered, you've been running a criminal information bureau out of a shithole café. It isn't a fucking community hub."

"I provide a service," Amelia corrected him. "Discreet. Reliable. And I charge a reasonable fee." She gestured with her chin towards Shank. "He's just a friend."

Shank said nothing.

George paced in front of them. "We know you went to the manor and stole the money from Floyd. Seeing as he didn't tell us about your café prior to all this, and neither did you, we'll be keeping the money as a punishment. It's an overdue payment. Protection money, for the privilege of operating your...establishment...on our Estate. We know it's a business. You sold our man here a cup of coffee earlier."

Amelia's shoulders slumped. There was no argument, no plea. Just acceptance.

She knew how the game was played.

George drove, Greg in the passenger seat. Shank and Amelia sat crammed in the back, wrists tied, blindfolds on. The black bag of cash, along with the suitcase, had been left at the warehouse. Moody had gone home.

George's mind strayed to Amelia. An old woman, seemingly harmless, running a lucrative intelligence network under the noses of everyone, including them. It was a masterstroke of disguise and cunning—her brainchild or Lenny's?

George glanced in the rearview mirror. Shank had dipped his head. Amelia sat upright on the wheel arch.

"You know," Greg said, "instead of being nice and giving you a slap on the wrist for lying about your skanky café and stealing cash, we could just make sure you both disappear. No witnesses, no loose ends."

Neither of them responded.

They drove for another ten minutes, then parked outside the café.

George cut the engine. "Right then. You've given us the money and explained your operation. We've taken what's owed, but you'll have to give us a cut in future. How much is to be discussed. Don't ever lie to us again, about anything, because if you do, the conversation won't be so polite."

Greg got out and opened the back door. "Get out."

They slowly extracted themselves from the back, and Greg untied their wrists and removed the blindfolds.

George wound down his window and called out, "There's one more thing, but we'll chat about that inside."

Amelia glanced at Shank, a silent exchange passing between them. He gave a slight nod. She unlocked the café door and stepped inside, Shank and the twins following close behind. Amelia switched the light on.

George stared at the streaky windows. "Get some fucking frosted shit for those."

"I've already suggested that," Shank said.

They sat around a table.

"Floyd," George prompted. "What else do you know about him?"

"He's always looking for a bigger bite," Amelia said. "He's been cultivating new alliances, trying to move up the ranks. He thinks he's clever. He's not." Her sly expression switched to a blank canvas. "He's been talking to some heavy hitters. The types who usually wouldn't give him the time of day."

George leaned forward, his interest piqued. "A job?"

"A shipment," Amelia said. "Pharmaceuticals. High-value. Not just the street stuff. This is the legitimate, controlled kind. Coming from a lab on the outskirts of Essex. It's due at the docks next week."

Pharmaceutical shipments. Legitimate ones were heavily regulated, monitored. Illegally diverted, they were worth a fortune. And if Floyd was involved, he was clearly out of his depth.

"Who's he working with?" Greg asked.

"I've gathered bits and pieces. Polish connections. A crew from the East End, and a consultant who used to work for the company handles the distribution."

"A consultant," George repeated. "Name?"

"Haven't got that yet. But I'm working on it. I hear things. Always do."

This old woman was a spider at the centre of a very intricate web.

"So, you're offering us this info because…?"

"A new arrangement. I don't pay protection money, but you get the intelligence, you get the opportunity to shut down menaces like Floyd."

George considered her, the audacity. She was offering them a potential goldmine and securing her future in the same breath.

George stood, Greg following suit.

"Keep your ears open," George said. "And if you hear anything else, you come to us directly. No more games. Understand?"

Amelia nodded. "Perfectly."

George couldn't shake the feeling that the old cow was up to something. The game had changed; Amelia had just shown them a new way to play. The past may be best left buried, as Shank had suggested, but the future, for Floyd at least, was about to be exposed.

Chapter Thirty

Misty rain hung in the air and wet the tarmac. Their van trundled along the road, George behind the wheel. He drove past a set of wrought-iron gates, the kind that screamed old money. Grove Manor, home to Floyd Fleece, a man who was becoming an increasingly irritating thorn in the twins' sides.

Out of the van, they marched to the front door. A couple of lights were on, despite the early hour. He thought about Floyd sending that message to let them know he'd watched Amelia and Shank huffing and puffing across the grass with his suitcase, entering the forest, then driving off. Why, so George and Greg wouldn't think he was some kind of mastermind behind a pharmaceutical job? Or was Amelia lying about that?

They didn't bother knocking. Greg produced a set of picks. The lock gave way, and they stepped inside. They checked the lower rooms. No one about, so they went upstairs. A light guided them, and they headed towards a room at the end of the landing. George pushed the door open, yellow light spilling into the landing. The room held nothing but a double bed, a table beside it, a half-empty glass on top, some clothes, and Floyd, tangled in sheets, his breathing punctuated by snores.

"Floyd!" George shouted.

Floyd bolted upright. His eyes, bleary with sleep and confusion, darted from side to side. Then he stared at the two figures standing by his bed.

"What the fuck?" His hand knocked the glass, sending it sailing. It landed on the floor but didn't smash, the fluid splashing out.

"Tell us about what's been going on," George said.

"Now? Christ…" He knuckled his eyes. "They thought they were clever, those two. Invited themselves here, saying they wanted to buy the house, then later, they fucking broke in and nicked the suitcase."

"A suitcase and cash you've apparently bragged about," Greg said.

"Stupid of me, but yeah, and I've regretted it ever since. They need to be taught a lesson. A harsh one."

George nodded. "Get dressed. We'll take you to them. A little trip to the warehouse, a friendly chat. You can confront them yourself."

Floyd clambered out of bed, shivering slightly in the nippy air. "Just let me…let me put on some clothes." He grabbed jeans and a top off a pile on the floor. As he dressed, he muttered to himself about the injustice and how dare two old fuckers trick him like that.

The drive was interesting. When encouraged to share more about himself, Floyd rambled on about the various schemes he'd dabbled in since he'd got out of the nick. Small-time cons, a persistent belief in himself to one day make it big, which he had in a way, via his brother's death. He painted Amelia and Shank as the ultimate betrayers, conveniently forgetting any of his own less-than-honourable dealings, not to mention he'd killed a teenager years ago.

"And when we get there," Floyd said, tapping George on the shoulder from the back of the van, "you make sure they understand. I want my money back, every single penny."

George wanted to gouge his eyes out for telling him what to do. Instead, he smiled in response, his focus fixed on the road. He hadn't bothered blindfolding Floyd, but the dickhead hadn't seemed to realise the significance of that. If he wasn't allowed to see the route, it meant he could go home, but if he *could* see it…

They drove out of the leafy suburbs and into an industrial area. The buildings grew grimmer, taller, concrete beasts.

George turned into the warehouse forecourt. "Here we are."

George and Greg went to the back of the van, and George opened the door.

Floyd hopped out, his confidence seeming to inflate. "So they're inside?"

They entered the warehouse, and George shut the door.

He looked at Floyd. "No, they aren't here."

Floyd swallowed. "What?"

"We're here to talk about *you*," George said. "More specifically, we're here to talk about a job you've got planned."

An expression of confusion crossed Floyd's face. "A job? What are you talking about? My only job is getting my money back from those conniving fuckers!"

"Don't play stupid, Floyd," Greg barked. "We know your plans. We know about the pharmaceuticals."

Floyd frowned. "Pharmaceuticals? What pharmaceuticals? I don't know anything about them." He genuinely seemed bewildered.

"You really are a piece of work, aren't you," George said. "We've got good intel."

Floyd's jaw dropped. "No, no, you've got it all wrong," he insisted, his voice rising in desperation. "I wouldn't... I couldn't... I've never even thought about doing a job like that. That's way out of my league."

George resisted walloping him one. "What's the plan? How were you going to get the shipment? Who's with you? Don't lie to me."

"I'm not lying!" Floyd cried. "I swear on my mother's life, I don't know what you're talking about."

Greg moved, a blur of motion. A heavy fist connected with Floyd's jaw, the crack of bone echoing. Floyd's head snapped back, his eyes watering, a trickle of blood appearing at the corner of his mouth. He groaned, bending over with his hands on his knees.

"Don't insult our intelligence," Greg said.

"I'm telling you the truth," Floyd sobbed, spitting out flecks of blood.

George looked at Greg, then back at Floyd who'd stood upright, cradling his jaw. There was something in his eyes: bafflement. He really didn't seem to know about the pharmaceutical job.

His denial felt too real.

Floyd whimpered. The man was a schemer, a loose cannon, a parasite on the fringes of their world. He talked too much, knew too many people, and now, he'd seen the route to their warehouse, understood their particular brand of justice from when they'd killed his brother. He was trouble, a liability.

"You know what, Floyd?" George said, so fucking tired of this shit. "It doesn't really matter whether you're doing a job or not."

Floyd's eyes widened. "No! Please! I told you the truth!"

Greg reached into his jacket, his hand emerging with a gun.

George sighed, thinking of the visit they'd have to make to Floyd's parents. They'd have to be made to see that keeping their mouths shut about two 'missing' sons really was the best way to go.

Chapter Thirty-One

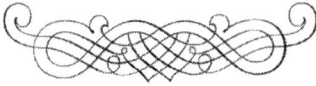

The wind scoured the exposed hillside. It whipped Amelia's black veil across her face, clawing at the netting, determined to reveal the mask beneath. She held the edge of it with one hand and clutched a white lily with the other—Lenny's favourite flower, or so everyone believed—and stared at the polished coffin. It was a dark, gleaming rectangle, almost as opaque and

unyielding as the man it contained. Forty-five years old, and Amelia stood at the graveside of her husband, at his charade of a funeral, on this bleak day in 1993.

Although it was far from bleak for her. She was fucking euphoric.

Around her, a sea of black suits rippled with the shifting wind. Men with suspicious eyes, their women with expressions of sorrow they didn't feel. Criminal mourners, every last one, gathered to pay their respects. Amelia wished she had the courage, just for a moment, to shed the veil so they saw the hate in her eyes when she screamed about who he really was. A monster. A viper. A walking, breathing darkness. But they wouldn't believe her. They'd likely think she was unhinged, consumed by grief, or worse, making a fool of herself.

So, she pretended. Squeezed out a tear or two.

Relief washed over her. He was gone. The weight that had pressed down on her for years had lifted.

The priest finished his platitudes. Earth hit the coffin with a dull thump, a sound that should have been final, but for Amelia, it merely marked the beginning of her new life. She dropped the lily onto the coffin. The pale petals contrasted sharply with the dark wood, a fleeting moment of beauty upon something that held someone so ugly.

As the mourners dispersed, forming small, hushed groups, a hand rested on Amelia's arm. Shank.

"I'll take you in my car," he said.

The procession to the wake was a sombre snake of black cars. Amelia stared out at the streets. They seemed different now. Or perhaps it was just her.

The wake was held at a function hall, the tables draped in dark velvet cloths and floral arrangements. The scent of lilies and cigar smoke got stuck in her throat. She stood by the open bar, holding a gin and tonic, and watched people, detached. They ate, they drank, they laughed, they commiserated. They told stories about Lenny Bagby, and with each anecdote, her stomach tightened, her blood pressure rising.

"He was a generous man." A big bloke raised his glass.

Amelia almost choked on her drink. Generous? He'd withheld money from her.

An elderly woman dabbed her eyes with a lace handkerchief. "Such a family man."

Amelia's grip on her glass tightened. Family man? If he could have got away with it, he'd have thrown a party when they'd lost their baby.

"He was shrewd, though," someone else said. "Never met a job Lenny couldn't make work for him. Smartest man I ever knew."

Smart, yes. But his intelligence was a weapon. He'd exploited weaknesses, widened the cracks in people's armour.

Shank approached her. "One thing Lenny told me about you that always stuck out. He said you kept him grounded."

What? She'd been the recipient of his manipulations. She was the one he could truly unleash his monster on, knowing she'd never speak about it, never leave, never betray. Because he'd made sure she had nowhere to go, no one to turn to. He'd isolated her completely. Even her own parents had shunned her in the end after he'd told them lies about her.

The urge to scream, to lash out, to rip off this grieving façade, pulsed through her veins. She imagined yelling, "He was an animal! He controlled my every breath! He took joy in my pain!" But the moment passed, a wave of rebellion that receded as quickly as it had come.

Shank must have sensed she wasn't in the mood, and he drifted away. Amelia watched him go, then turned to stare at the portrait of Lenny hanging on the wall above the buffet table. She remembered the last few months, the slow decline. He'd fought it with the same ferocity he'd fought everything else, but this was a battle even Lenny Bagby couldn't win.

Amelia had performed her duties: arranging his medication, cooking meals, listening to his bullshit stories. But inside, a dark, secret joy had blossomed. Each cough was a victory. Each day that cancer ate him alive, a little more of her soul and spirit returned.

She finished her drink, placed the empty glass on a passing tray, and walked towards the exit. She didn't need to stay. She'd played her part. Shank would take care of the rest, probably telling everyone she was too distraught to remain. The mourners would continue to glorify Lenny's memory, believing the myth.

As she stepped out, away from the cloying sweetness of lilies, she smiled.

Her world had been reset. She was ready to begin again.

Chapter Thirty-Two

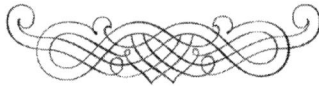

The memory of the funeral always made her smile. Such a shame that she hadn't really begun again, like she'd thought she would. She'd continued to run the café, even down to keeping it grotty like Lenny wanted. The only difference was that no man told her what to do anymore. She hadn't even allowed the twins to, hence her making a deal—no protection money, just information. Her rules.

Amelia pulled a steaming mug of coffee towards her. She had a while to think about what she was going to do now she didn't have that money. She could still move away, it just meant she wouldn't have as much money to live on. Not that she expected to live that much longer, ten years if she was extremely lucky, so maybe it was an option.

It wasn't as if she planned to live like a queen.

If there was one thing she could thank Lenny for, it was how she'd learned to lie at the drop of a hat. The bullshit story about Floyd doing a job had come to her without much thought, and she couldn't give a shit whether she'd thrown him under the bus. She'd also done it to show Shank how you treated someone you cared about. You didn't walk away when the going got tough, you stood up straighter and proved your worth. Going by the look he'd sent her way for saving his arse, he understood exactly what she'd done and why.

She wasn't going to open the café today. She'd been up all night, thinking things through, and she was so exhausted she needed to get some sleep.

A tap sounded on the door, and she had a feeling she knew who it was. Shank. His arrival was as predictable as the sun rising. Even though she was desperate for her bed, she got up to let him in. She had no worries about leaving him down here when she when upstairs. He might even open up for her, save her losing any fee money.

He stood in the doorway, his eyes red-rimmed. He looked bloody knackered. He never said anything, just came in and sat at his usual table. He'd changed clothes, probably had a shower, although his checked shirt was rumpled, his hair dishevelled. He reminded her of a man frazzled by disappointment.

She made him a coffee and sat opposite.

"Morning," he said.

"Morning," Amelia replied.

She wanted to talk to him about the twins but at the same time couldn't be bothered. They'd made the Estate their kingdom, and they weren't going to let mere subjects tell them how to run things. She was half expecting them to make an appearance today, telling her they'd had a think and now refused her offer of information instead of protection money.

At least now she didn't have to keep up the condensation bollocks. They knew the café existed, so there was no need to hide, but then again, she had to cater to her customers. Maybe she'd concede and put up the frosted covering so the criminals at least had some semblance of privacy.

Until she sold up, that was.

The door burst inwards with a splintering crash that had her screaming out in fright and jumping to her feet. A gust of icy air swept through, gripping Amelia's newspaper and tossing it around. Two figures, cloaked in black, stepped inside, balaclavas hiding their faces. Before Shank could lift his head more than an inch from his cup, they moved.

The first strode directly towards their table. He raised a hand, a gun held firm. There was no warning, no shouted demand, just a *pfft-pfft* as two rounds tore through the air. Shank's head slumped forward, smacking onto the table. His cup remained upright next to his lifeless hand.

Dead. Just like that.

Amelia couldn't grasp it. It was too fast, too sudden. Her Shank. Gone.

As her brain struggled to process the violence, the second masked man turned his attention to her, his gun aimed. She didn't even have time to scream. The *pfft-pfft* again, and a searing pain erupted in her chest that drove the air from her lungs. She stumbled backwards, collapsing against the far wall then sliding down to the floor. A harsh ache spread through her, sapping her strength. Her vision blurred, the familiar shapes of her café twisting and warping. The copper tang of blood filled her mouth. She pressed her palm to the wound, her fingers becoming slick and warm. This was it. This was the way she was going to go out.

She struggled to draw breath and watched them.

They removed their balaclavas.

Amelia focused every ounce of her remaining will to see. The faces that emerged were familiar. Hard eyes and set jaws. Faces devoid of emotion.

George smiled at her. "You lied to us. About Floyd."

The Brothers shared a look. A nod. George pulled a clear plastic bottle from his jacket pocket, its contents sloshing. He removed the lid. Petrol. He splashed it over the counter, the tables, over Shank's body. Greg produced a box of matches and lit one, its small flame wavering.

Bitter rage mingled with the creeping cold in Amelia's limbs. Her café. Her home. Reduced to ashes soon.

The first flames roared to life with a hungry whoosh. Orange and red tongues licked greedily, crawling rapidly up the walls. The heat, even from her position on the floor, was intense. Smoke billowed upwards, stinging her eyes, filling her lungs.

George and Greg walked calmly towards the door.

Through the tears in her eyes, Amelia watched them go. Their silhouettes, framed against the rapidly growing blaze, paused for a moment at the doorway, then melted into the grey anonymity of the street.

The flames were everywhere now. They danced on the counter, leaped across the tables, turned the old wooden chairs into crackling infernos. The smell of burning wood, burning memories, filled her nostrils.

Her last sight, before the smoke claimed her vision entirely, before the pain became too great, was of the flames. They rose higher and higher, a roaring orange tide, devouring. They shot towards her, their hungry mouths open wide, ready to eat her whole, leaving no trace of the woman who'd never felt truly loved.

Chapter Thirty-Three

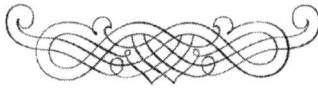

George stood outside the café, the interior an orange square through the window that would blow out anytime soon. Greg stood beside him, apparently indifferent to the fact they'd gunned down an old geezer and shot an old lady, leaving her to choke and burn to death. This was a message, he'd said, to all the fuckers who'd sat in there and plotted.

George had looked Amelia in the eye just before he'd shot her. He remembered the brief flash of terror, the sudden horror as he'd raised the gun.

He shrugged. "Time to go."

Greg nodded, already turning towards their van. Its bland anonymity was their greatest asset. As George got in the driver's seat, the flashing glow of the burning café was reflected in the rearview mirror, a pulsing heart of destruction in the morning dark.

George navigated the streets, taking a convoluted route home. The cityscape blurred past, a collage of lit windows, neon signs, and trees.

"You're quiet," Greg said.

"Just thinking."

"About what?"

"Shank."

Greg sighed. "He was collateral damage. A regrettable necessity. He chose to side with her, George."

"I know."

"That's how it works. You get entangled, you face the consequences."

George pushed a hand through his hair. The scent of smoke still clung to his clothes. "It just felt wrong this time."

They drove in silence for a while. George caught a glimpse of their reflection in the darkened window of a passing bus. Two men, identical in build, expressionless, driving a nondescript van through London. Who would suspect them? Who would ever guess what they'd just done?

They arrived home. Greg was out of the van first. Indoors, Greg went straight for the living room. George followed, peeling off his smoke-tinged clothes and putting them in the fireplace. Greg would set them alight.

George went upstairs. He stepped under the scalding shower spray, letting the water sluice over his skin, trying to wash away more than sweat. He scrubbed at his hair, as if he could scour the memory of Amelia and Shank from his mind. The heat stung, but the chill of guilt remained for gunning down that old man.

But like Greg had said, Shank was dangerous. Even with the café burned to the ground, he'd have set the community hub up elsewhere. They'd still have had the problem to deal with— once they'd found where it was.

He saw Amelia's face again, eyes framed by the sudden, brief terror, then the slackness of approaching death.

Fuck it.

George got out and dressed. His phone beeped, and the screen showed a snippet of a message from Colin. George opened it, sighing.

COLIN: I'VE GOT TWO BODIES AT A WAREHOUSE, ONE INSIDE, ONE OUTSIDE. YOUNG LADS. ONE OF THEM IS PRESTON ROBINS, AND THE OTHER IS RILEY SMITH. ANYTHING TO DO WITH YOU?

GG: NOPE.

COLIN: WHAT ABOUT A NAME ON BOTH OF THEIR PHONES. THEY RECEIVED MESSAGES FROM SOMEONE CALLED SHANK, ASKING THEM TO MEET AT THE WAREHOUSE.

George's guilt about killing the old man suddenly evaporated.

GG: YEAH, THAT'S LOOSELY LINKED TO US, BUT WE DIDN'T KILL THOSE LADS, HE MUST HAVE.

COLIN: ANY IDEA WHERE I CAN FIND HIM?

GG: HIS BURNT AND SHOT BODY IS IN A CAFÉ ALONG WITH AN OLD WOMAN. THEY'RE OURS.

COLIN: WHY DIDN'T YOU WARN ME?

GG: BECAUSE WE'VE BEEN TOO FUCKING BUSY.

He put the phone in his pocket and went downstairs to get Ralph, their dog, out of his crate, reminding himself that they'd have to get rid of their guns. Ralph lifted his head, a low rumble of greeting emanating from his chest. His tail wagged.

"All right, mate?" George scratched him behind the ears. "Ready for a walk?"

The early morning air was sharp and cold. The bloody rain fell again, misting the streetlights. Ralph trotted ahead, tugging gently on the lead.

They walked to a field behind the house. While Ralph ran around, George let his mind wander, the images of the café fire receding slightly, replaced by the quiet rhythm of the world waking up, the horizon gaining a light-grey hue. He found a strange solace in this routine, a brief respite from the relentless tension of his life.

Back at the house, Greg was already in bed. George went up to his, Ralph following. He circled a few times before collapsing on his fluffy donut with a contented sigh. George knelt and stroked the dog's head, feeling the warmth of his fur, the steady beat of his heart.

He stood by the window, looking out at the rain. Somewhere out there, the remnants of the café would be smouldering, a crime scene being meticulously processed. The news channels would pick it up, a tragic accident—until the bullets were discovered.

George pulled the curtains across, plunging the room into darkness. He climbed into bed, the mattress dipping under his weight, and closed his eyes.

Things would look better when he woke up.

Chapter Thirty-Four

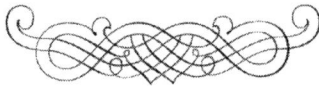

The December wind was an unwelcome companion that buffeted James' threadbare coat and clawed at the exposed skin of his neck. London wasn't the city of glistening skyscrapers and booming businesses, not for him, nor for Max or Todd. For them, it was an expanse of concrete filled with people indifferent to their issues.

He'd discovered a lot of people didn't like the homeless.

They'd been walking for hours, the scuff of their worn boots on the ground a reminder of their exhaustion. Miles stretched behind them, receding streetlights and the distant, ceaseless hum of traffic. Each of them carried the weight of their life on their backs: a rucksack, lumpy with the essentials, a tent, the cherished sleeping bag. Their destination, a sparse copse of trees at the edge of the forest.

"Not long," Max said.

Todd didn't speak. James often wondered what demons danced in his quiet moments, but he never asked. On the streets, questions were often an invitation for trouble, and even though the three of them had decided to stick together, they didn't know each other that well.

James' thoughts were a droning whinge about the cold, hunger, and the ache in his hips, knees, and feet. He focused instead on the familiar ritual of placing one foot in front of the other. The city sprawl had given way to a more rural landscape. Overgrown hedges, tall trees.

Just as the last sliver of twilight bled from the sky, Todd stopped abruptly. Max almost walked into his back. James, a few paces behind, halted, his gaze following Todd's fixed stare. Through a thinning screen of ancient oaks stood a house. No, not a house. A manor.

They trudged up the gravel driveway. A jolt of unease went through James. An open front door, in a place like this, was an invitation, but also a warning. Should they risk going inside? The cold was burrowing deep, and the thought of pitching a tent on frozen ground held little appeal.

"Could be a squat," Todd said.

Curiosity, a dangerous but compelling force, warred with James' ingrained caution. The lure of shelter was a strong pull.

No lights within, no signs of life. The door must have been left open for a while as leaves had blown in.

Max approached first. He peered in. "Hello?" He took a step inside, then another.

Fuck this. James followed, his senses on high alert. The air inside was still and cold, carrying the scent of the outdoors.

"Bloody hell," Todd whispered behind them. "It's fucking massive."

They moved through the ground floor, cautious intruders, their footsteps loud. It felt less like a squat and more like someone had gone out and not come back. The lack of furniture was weird.

"No one's here," James said.

Max pointed to a doorway beside a bookcase and the slice of stairs visible through the gap. "Cellar? Might be a good place to kip. Out of sight. No windows for anyone to see us from outside."

A cellar offered a sense of security, of being truly hidden. They shut the front door and went down the stone staircase, the air growing colder.

"Fuck me," Max said. "This is like a flat. The steel bars are a bit much, though."

James looked around. "And the cages around the beds. What the hell went on here?"

But the beds had mattresses, and pillows and blankets. It was heaven compared to what they'd been used to.

"But it'll do." Max pulled his rucksack from his shoulders and put it on the floor beside a sofa.

James and Todd did the same. The simple act of shedding their burdens, of knowing they wouldn't be moving again for a few hours, at least, was a luxury. They ate their food, showered in the bathroom beside the bedrooms, then sat on the sofas in the dark under blankets.

Then, Todd said, "I've got something to tell you. It's been bugging me for ages, keeping it quiet."

"What is it?" James asked.

"I've killed someone."

James froze. He thought he'd misheard, perhaps a trick of his exhausted mind.

Max let out a choked sound. "What did you say?"

"I killed someone. My first, I didn't mean to. Not really. It just…happened."

James wanted to laugh, to dismiss it as a sick joke, but there was no tremor in Todd's voice, no hint of a lie.

"Your…first?" Max said. "What the hell are you talking about?"

Todd sighed. "There've been others. After the first, it gets…easier. You get better at it. At making sure they don't find out. At making sure they don't find them."

They? The police?

"You're fucking about, right?" Max asked. "You're just trying to scare us."

"Nope. I'm not joking."

James wanted to run, but where? They were in a weird cellar, miles from anywhere. What if Todd wasn't just confessing?

What if we're next?

To be continued in *Random*,
The Cardigan Estate 47

Printed in Dunstable, United Kingdom